Drawn by the faint, meandering so
flute from deep in misty English v
clerk in a northern provincial town, discovers Joe, a middle-aged
Navajo Indian with a life-hardened experience of failed marriages
and addictions. Their unlikely meeting, challenging both age and
culture, kindles an edgy yet mutual passion, entwined with the
acting-out of a contemporary Arthurian drama set against a wild
Northumbrian landscape of myth and legend, leading to fateful
consequences for both their lives.

Other titles by the author

A Twist in Coyote's Tale
The Fourth Gateway
Simply Totem Animals (Zambezi Publishing 2010)

for full details of all our books please visit our website

archivepublishing.co.uk
and
transpersonalbooks.com

A Dark Wind

Celia M Gunn

ARCHIVE
publishing

This revised and expanded edition of
A Dark Wind
by
Archive Publishing
Dorset, England

© Celia M Gunn 2005, 2009

The rights of Celia M Gunn as author have been asserted
in accordance with the Copyrights, Designs and Patents Act 1988.

A CIP Record for this book is available from
The British Cataloguing in Publication data office

ISBN 978-1-906289-11-9 (Paperback)

First published in 2005

Designed at Archive Publishing by Ian Thorp

Cover illustration by Yuri Leitch

Printed and bound by
Lightning Source

What is it that we are part of? And what is it that we are?

Robin Williamson, "The Half-Remarkable Question"
Wee Tam, The Incredible String Band, 1968.

For Anthony

ONE

Dilute, haloed, the sun hangs over the abbey, illuminating the pitted sandstone with an otherworldly light. In the fold of the valley below, the rimed fields are empty, skeletal trees crowding at their edge. Like a hunted creature crouched holding its breath, the misted woods are still. There is no sound, not even of a bird.

A dark, hooded figure slips out of the shadowy trees. Leaning on a staff, it moves slowly and silently along the prickling hedgerow. Suddenly it stops, motionless as a tree-stump.

With a resonant thundering, a horse appears over the crest of the hill above the woods. Urged by its rider, it careers down along their edge, mane and tail streaming, mouth foam-flecked, ears back, eyes wild and white, as if fearful of what follows its headlong flight.

Unsheathed, a sword glints dully in the rider's gloved hand. Wrapped tight about his body, pinned by an elaborate silver brooch, his midnight-blue cloak is darkened with a shining wet stain. His dark hair is gathered and tied at the back of his neck; a heavy moustache hides his mouth. He leans into the neck of his mount to hasten its progress.

Or perhaps for support.

Hooves ringing on the frozen, unforgiving earth, the war-horse seems to take heart as the heavy wooden gate of the abbey creaks open. It surges up the slope, passing swift and strong between massive beeches, blackened by age and storm, which mark an ancient causeway to the sacred place. Reaching the dark maw in the thick stone wall, the animal rears and snorts, misting the air with steaming hot breath, and plunges inside.

Scolding rooks lift and swirl in the wintry air like tea-leaves as the gates grind closed.

With the ceasing of the crashing, reckless passage, the shadow by the hedgerow begins to move again. Its cloak is tattered, the hood pulled over its face. It is stooped; perhaps from age or against the bitter cold. Slowly it begins to make its way up to the abbey.

"Cut! Cut! Yeah, that about wraps it up," Jess yelled, waving his baseball cap wildly, as if to remind everyone who was in control.

Camera Two had the better angle of the abbey. Standing behind the camera-man, Joe nodded gently, feeling a warm glow. It had worked just as he'd imagined it, although the unexpected appearance and rasping calls of the black birds had spooked him.

"Waste of fuckin' time and money, bringin' in extras today," Jess added loudly to no-one in particular, pulling his cap back over his cropped fair hair, his small, deep eyes glittering and icy as stars.

Joe held still, telling himself the birds did not have to be an omen. The director always acted as if his failed guidance was someone else's fault, usually anyone out of earshot, but he knew better than to cross him; there was no telling what Jess might do in return. In any case, whatever he said, the day would slide downhill from this point on. Jess didn't like being upstaged.

Maybe better to say nothing, he thought; but sometimes, to keep the peace, words were called for. "Next shot," he offered, "put some of 'em to work outside the abbey. It'd add texture. Gatherin' firewood ... whatever peasants do...." Watching Jess stalk away without a word, Joe shrugged, thrusting his hands deep into the copious pockets of his overcoat.

If people would take the time before working in a new place, he thought. Study it, talk about their vision....

"Hey, Joe, whatcha doin' with that gun in your hand?"

Deep in thought, he hadn't noticed Melanie behind him. Her sing-song rendition of the old Hendricks' hit was a time-worn joke; he wished she'd quit.

"Don't mind the ol' sourpuss," she added with a laugh. "We all know who came up with it, and you were right: not having serfs milling about, choking up the shot, gave it a much greater impact."

Instinctively, Joe assessed the distance between the words and Jess's departing back. Melanie had a way of choosing her moment, and the last thing anyone needed was for the director to overhear; it would be salt rubbed in his festering ego. Still, he knew well what motivated her.

Heavy lips pursed, Melanie tossed her thick, dark hair and briefly cast her eyes down, then up at him, her fine eyebrows arched. She tended to do this, Joe had learned. To him, it looked as if she were in perpetual surprise, but he guessed it was her way of making her eyes look more appealing. Or maybe she did it to seem sympathetic. They shared difficulties: the director's arrogance and his unconscious stealing of others' creativity, and other irritating habits. She was expecting him to commiserate. But what was the point, when these were forces over which he had no control? With a nod of acknowledgment, Joe chose instead to turn away. He headed down to the hooded figure, now being fussed over by a make-up girl.

The old actor threw back his hood as Joe approached, revealing long, wispy white hair, a pale, sharp-featured face lattice-worked with wrinkles, a beard stubbled white, and rheumy blue eyes which seemed more watery than ever, as if he were about to weep.

Owen's voice cracked like a whiplash. "Should put you at the helm more often, my boy. These old bones appreciate it."

Joe shrugged. "It was you. The books you loaned me. The places you took me."

"Hah!" grunted the old man. "Don't think I haven't noticed that every time you take the reins, a single shot and it's in the bag. I'd lend you my whole library if it meant I didn't have to do those damn interminable rounds of retakes your boss is so partial to. But all the books in the world won't do more than provide a framework. Can't educate for an eye. Or for imagination. Either you have it or you don't."

Imagination.... The epic tales had filled Joe's head with the clash of battle and the howl of war-cry, the towering presence of great stone castles and abbeys, the courage and vision of heroes, of kings, knights and magicians, and the rustle of ancient, haunted forests. He had been transported into the lore of the land, a land unlike any he'd known. Cloaked in mist, washed dull with rain, damp and cold. The daily struggle of the weakened sun was almost painful to witness. Yet the sense of a singular purpose, of a great, far-reaching vision, of a raw and mystical power, had made him unaccountably nostalgic.

He wanted to tell the old man something about remembering what it is to dream, but the words were hard to find. In any case, in his usual way, the actor had already silently dismissed both Joe and the girl with a wave of his arm, and was walking away.

Letting whiteman get too close was usually painful and costly, Joe remembered, watching Owen's progress towards the trailers. There was no trace of the bent, pained elder in his loping stride. When he paused to light a cigarette, the faint swirl of blue smoke in his wake reminded Joe of an earlier idea he'd had, an unusual angle for the next shot. He turned to go back up the hill to check it out, but something made him stop and look over the whole site.

The vehicles and trailers looked almost like something out of an old Western, gathered in a tight knot as if ready to ward off an Indian raid. Canvas awnings stretched between the trailers and a coach, a makeshift attempt to provide additional shelter for equipment as much as people, and most of the crew were down there now, making the most of the swift completion and taking a coffee-break. Ray was adjusting lighting equipment, thick cables snaking blackly away to the generator, where Jess was standing having a head-to-head with Mark, Melanie about to join them. Unneeded and unheeded, the extras were gathered in a disconsolate, shabby-looking cluster in the lee of a ruined wall of the old abbey.

Despite his heavy overcoat, Joe shivered. His right side ached, an old injury made worse by the dampness. He stared at the broken tower, the tumbled blocks of stone, and thought about the hundreds of years of prayer and meditation that permeated them, and the lingering vibration of long-ago pain. Unbidden, an image of one of the old, life-size stone sculptures within the walls came back to haunt him: a robed monk, hands pressed together and raised high, fingers jutting skywards; bare head tipped back, cheeks stretched hollow by a mouth agape in anguish, blind stone eyes straining at the heavens. Silent agony, forever preserved.

A sudden, urgent need to have done with this place, these people, overtook Joe. A sort of panic gripped him; his hands started to shake. Underneath, he felt a familiar, deep-seated churning and closed his eyes against its insistence.

Halfway across the globe. The passage of miles made no more difference than the passing of time.

Hunched against the cold, Kathy felt as if she were shrinking into the hard earth. The soles of the ill-fitting, worn old footwear they'd been given were thin as cardboard and her feet had lost all sensation. The peasant's outfit she was wearing smelled musty and chafed at her neck and, despite being layered, was shockingly useless against the cold. Turning to her friend, who was dressed in a similar way, she blew into her fingers, rubbed her hands together and stamped moodily.

"If I'd've known we'd have to stand round for hours waiting, I could've worn me Nan's winter woollies," she grumbled, pulling at the threadbare jacket. "Nobody would have known underneath this stupid outfit. 'S bloody freezing. I've never got up so early to get paid for doing nowt."

"Bunch of fuckin' sadists," Emily agreed.

A heavy-set, long-haired youth who'd been hanging round them since they'd got off the bus took the opportunity to get closer to them.

"Last thing them lot'll think of is us, hinny." His Northumbrian accent was strong. "But I'll borrer yer me hoodie. Kept it on, under, so's it'll be warm, like." He began to pull off his peasant smock.

Kathy wrinkled her nose. "Euchh ... don't bother." She let all her feelings out in the slurred words.

"Divvent ye torn yer nose up at me, hen," the lad said tightly.

"Hen! You go lay an egg." Kathy grabbed Emily's arm and pulled her away. She hated being called "hen". And getting chatted up by a local lad, who was probably a farm-worker or a labourer by the looks of him, was not why she was here. But neither had she come to stand round and freeze. Never one for getting up early – it had still been pitch-dark outside – she was fed up with the interminable waiting and hated how fat and ugly she knew she must look in the coarse, bulky clothes. And being constantly aware of how awful her hair looked, because they'd been told not to wash it, made her feel even worse. She swiped at her cold nose, which was another worry: she knew it had to be reddened.

Fat chance of being discovered, looking like this, she thought angrily.

"Hurry up, and wait," she grumbled. "Go here, go there, all for nothing. What're we supposed to be doing now? Oh, that's Russell Brandon down there again, isn't it?" Reluctant to take her hands out of the warmth of her armpits, she nudged Emily, pointing with her chin. But even the sight of a major film-star didn't soften her mood. "Unbelievable. They actually used a stand-in to ride the horse, did you see that? Can't get over how he looks, when you see him for real. God, he's effing ancient. How can Julie Noble play opposite him? There's not enough money ... imagine having to kiss him. Or even ... yuck, the thought of him with no clothes on." She managed a giggle and theatrical shiver at the same time. Or maybe it was from the chill. "I hope they use a body-double for the sexy bits. Honestly, you'd think they could've cast someone better. She's so beautiful; as if she'd find someone like him attractive. And it's so stupid," she lengthened the word, trying for an American accent, "an American as Lancelot. I mean, how-"

"Brandon was good in 'Starforce Nine'," Emily broke in. "He played a Russian cosmonaut in that. He does good accents."

For some reason, Emily's tone heightened Kathy's irritation. "Don't remember. Anyway, bet he can't do a proper English one. Why couldn't they use someone English? We've got plenty of great actors over here. Even up here in the north, although them nobs from down south think we're all barbarians.... As for using what's-'is-name for Merlin-"

"It'll be to do with the American market. It's their production, after all. Brandon's got pulling power over there; here, too. At least they got Julie Noble. And you've got to agree Owen Robinson's doesn't half look the part. You'd expect Merlin to look like that, ancient and creepy. And he's good. He's been in theatre all his life; he's a Shakespearean-"

"Has-been, duh! I know!" Kathy scathingly interrupted, watching the old man flamboyantly sweep back his cloak and walk away, leaving the make-up girl with her brush waving in the air and the tall, dark man – some kind of big-wig as far as she could tell – just standing there, looking sort of lost, discarded.

Serves him right, she thought. I hope he does get lost, then maybe we could all go home. But she kept the thought to herself and remained silent, watching him.

She'd noticed him earlier, shortly after they'd arrived. At the time, she'd thought he had to be one of the actors; someone she hadn't heard of, but who clearly had something of a presence. For some reason, she hadn't pointed him out to her friend, though. Dark, lean, and quite different and intense-looking, he walked with the smooth grace of a dancer, holding himself very straight. And even if his tan, and his little pony-tail and black hat were a bit of an affectation, there was something about him that caught and held her eye.

If they had to have an American, she thought, he'd have made a good Lancelot.

She turned to Emily. "Funny how in the movies, actresses always have to be young and beautiful, while actors ... well, they're not all old and ugly, but it doesn't seem to matter much if they are."

"Brandon's got charisma, hadn't you noticed? Honestly, Kathy, just shut up, or at least don't be such a fucking misery-guts. We're all in the same boat. What did you expect?"

Kathy shook her head, choosing dignified silence. Emily was such a pain; she knew fine well. This was the chance of a lifetime. It had been all they'd talked about ever since they'd heard about it. Brushing up against film-stars, producers, directors, anything could happen. They'd dreamed up greater things: how Hollywood might even come calling. She knew she was attractive, enough people had commented. Although she ought to lose some weight. But her eyes were large and a startling Viking-blue, her mouth a generous and symmetrical curve, and she had her Dad's cheekbones. Her long, ash-blonde hair was its natural colour; and she loved her graceful neck and prominent collar-bones. And she had one over on Emily (who was stick-thin and actually dreamed of being a model), because she was the one with a flair for acting.

"Drama queen," her Nan had used to call her, and not unkindly. Super-excited by the opportunity, she'd come here ready to put heart and soul into it, positive she'd stand out, given the chance. And it had come just at the right time. For months she'd been fed up with life in a small market town, but didn't know what to do about it. Getting enough money together to move, down to Newcastle for example, seemed impossible. She felt she'd come to a point where if something didn't happen soon, she'd go mad.

Or do something to make it happen.

Only what "it" was, Kathy had no idea. Except that something had to give, she could feel it. It was like being caged, being locked into someone else's idea of what her life should be about.

But this wasn't turning out to be any kind of opportunity at all. The lowly wardrobe girls had treated them like cattle. Mark, who'd been funny and charming and seemed to really like her when he'd taken down their details at the Job Centre, telling her she might even get a line or two and then wouldn't be just an extra but a supporting actor, hadn't even acknowledged her since they'd arrived at the site. But, watching him this morning, she'd seen he was just a very small fish, not some important casting director like she'd imagined, and her hope of being given a line had swiftly evaporated as she realised there was a distinct hierarchy. As for getting on friendly terms with the lighting camera-man, whom she'd read was the most important person on the set, none of the crew took the slightest notice of the lowly extras. And she'd soon found out it was no use trying to catch the eye of any of them; they were all too caught up in their own self-importance. Then she'd overheard one of the minor actors saying that if a person were serious about acting, they'd never take on work as an extra because it blocked further opportunities.

Cold and frustrated, she thought how cosy-warm it would be at the bank and how there wouldn't have been much to do, given that it was the quietest time of the month. It seemed stupid now to have sacrificed two precious days of annual leave to stand and freeze out here in the pathetic hope of something earth-changing happening in her life. Probably no-one would even notice if she left. Remembering Mark saying the food was good and that there was loads of it, she decided to stay for the free lunch then sneak away. It was a couple of miles back to town, but she'd probably manage to hitch a ride. Although she'd walk if she had to.

The little glade offered a privacy and peace he'd been looking for without knowing it. Joe found a spot where the sun could reach and sat down on a cushion of dead leaves, crossed his legs and leaned back against a convenient mossy log. From his pocket, he produced a small leather pouch from which he took out a pinch of tobacco, premixed with some weed, and a leaf of cigarette paper. Expertly, he rolled a slim joint. The air was crisp but his coat was warm, and here he could feel a faint touch of sun-warmth on his face as he smoked.

Black columns, the trees rose round him, their branches stark against the colourless sky. Meditatively he traced their outline with his eyes, acquainting himself with their leafless reach and stretch. Great brown lips of fungus pouted from wounds in the trunks. Other dark-green, sinister growths sprouted from the rot he could smell all about him. The warmth of the milky sun was a soft, moist kiss on his skin.

It was never good to smoke, it hurt the lungs, but sometimes it was necessary. For a while he closed his eyes, immersing himself in the lightening, the distancing sensation.

But the smell, leaking through ... always the cold mouldering dampness of this decaying, crowded little island....

Imagining a time when it had been covered with forest brought his memory to the place in the south where the shooting had begun. The New Forest, they called it. Even now, it made him chuckle. Having assumed the name to be another example of the irony that laced the English humour, he'd been put straight by Owen: wave after wave of invasion; the settlements and introduction of agriculture; the gradual erosion of the great forests that had once covered the whole island; and the forgetting of the sacred groves and the ancient tree-religion.

It had been a powerful thing to learn about, this fore-runner to his own race's recent history. Joe's innate repulsion for the Europeans' blatant disrespect for and misuse of the land which gives life had been somehow tempered, when he understood that they had done it to their own land, before they did it to the New World; that their lack of respect for his own people's way of life had precedence among themselves. Somehow, somewhere along the line, whiteman had become so fearful of nature that he thought he could control it; he had forgotten that he could only ever be but one weak entity in the overall plan of the master forces of nature.

Half-mad, half-genius, the old actor had enlightened Joe in ways that he deeply appreciated. Owen was very different: self-obsessed and neurotic – in short, an actor – but sharp-minded and self-deprecating, and not restless like most whites, who could not keep still when they talked, who swiftly changed their facial expression. Grandfather, he might have called him, if they had come across each other in another time, another place. Although he knew to keep distance from strong people, so as not to be mastered by them.

Early on, Owen had insisted on taking him to visit the ancient places: the mounded burial-places of prehistoric kings, the great circles of standing stones. Now mere greening humps returning to nature, but set aside, as was only right, the burial-mounds were not to be approached. But the standing stones were a powerful, unforgettable statement. Thousands of years, marking the patterning of the stars, Owen had said. Joe wondered what had been in their mind, the people who had raised them; why they might wish for those who came after to see exactly as they saw. So long ago, tearing apart the land to make such a lasting statement, written in stone....

Gazing inwardly, Joe returned to the myth that had brought him across the ocean, conjuring up an age of fiercely-proud tribal peoples, their lives ruled and ordered by kings and magicians. Lowly huts of straw and mud, and great halls of stone, dim and smoky within. The clash of tempered metal, of sword and spear. The betrayal of cloak and dagger. A time of dignity and honour, when power and fate and destiny had knitted a whole land together and brought it to its zenith. The vision of one great man had brought unity, yet it was for but a mere blink in the eye of time.

Joe considered how whiteman's destiny seemed always the same; how their history turned in ever-repeating circles, as if they'd never moved on from their wrathful, controlling Old Testament god. He wondered if that were a pattern in itself. Now that he was no longer trying to be like whiteman, it was as if he could see them more clearly. Maybe their distance from him – when he thought of it – was part of their nature, their beauty, their pattern. For a moment, he felt sympathy, and then shame as he remembered he was hating the whiteman part of himself.

The deep sense of weariness returned. Nipping out the joint, Joe wrapped it in a damp leaf and put it in his pocket, then sat with his face turned up to the sun, his mind empty.

After several minutes, he started involuntarily, as if someone had touched him.

There was no-one. Only the silent, witnessing trees. Reaching into an inner pocket, he took out his flute and breathed softly into its familiarity, warming it, then began enticing from it soft notes, like falling snowflakes meandering through the bare branches of the trees. His fingers grew cold, but his body burned. He played out his song, a yearning from somewhere beyond him, about a lost time and a lost land. Spinning out the ache of his own loss, never pausing, and ignoring the faint crackle of brittle twig and leaf behind him.

Unsure what to do next, Kathy kept still. Having informed Emily of her escape-plan, she'd left her in the catering coach, planning to sneak into the wardrobe tent to change. But first she'd had to make a rather pressing visit to the loo. It was from there, on the outermost edge of the site, that she'd heard the faint, tuneless, weaving sound, of some kind of flute. Slowly spreading, it was the saddest sound she had ever heard anyone make. It seemed full of messages, making her think of cold white moonlight and howling dogs, and she'd felt compelled to find its source. The search took her down to the edge of the woods.

Before coming across the dark figure sitting on the bare earth, playing the flute, she smelled the sharp-sweet tang of cannabis and almost changed her mind, but curiosity – or something deeper, a sort of Pied Piper effect, she would later think – led her on.

The flute-player's back was to her, but the black hat and pony-tail gave away his identity. Thrilled to have stumbled accidentally across one of the important people on the set, especially when he was on his own, at the same time, she felt like she was intruding. Clearly he hadn't heard her approaching; the music was unbroken, barely audible in the still, cold air. If it could be called music. There was no melody, just an eerie, sad, wandering sound that was starting to give her goose-pimples.

It seemed like the moment she decided to creep away again, he stopped playing and glanced over his shoulder at her.

"Wench. Someone send you to find me? They startin' up again?"

The old English word sounded incongruous with an American intonation, but his accent was somehow not quite American. Kathy felt her face grow warm, and looked down, scuffing at the rotting leaves with her battered leather costume-boot.

"What? Oh, no. I'm just one of the extras. I heard the music ... I mean, your flute, and just followed the sound...." She broke off. He had to know she'd smelled the cannabis and was probably thinking she wanted to have a toke. And more: people like him had to be hounded by groupies, just like rock stars were. Or by someone looking for the big break.

But was this her chance?

She looked straight at him. He wasn't quite looking at her, however, and he was scowling, a deep line etched between his dark, angled brows. His face was narrow with high cheek-bones, and deeply tanned, which looked strange for the time of year. But for a strange little bump, his nose was long and straight. She guessed it had probably been broken some time in the past. His lips were slim and sensual, and down-turned; his chin jutted like a rock. He looked angry, but, knowing from experience that people weren't always aware of the expression on their face, she wasn't particularly bothered. His eyes were faintly almond-shaped and dark like deep pools, and when he suddenly looked directly at her, she was disconcerted by the feeling he was seeing inside her somehow. She shivered.

"I've never seen.... What kind of flute is that?" Kathy regretted the childish question as soon as it crossed her lips, but she had to say something.

Looking down at the instrument in his hand, he shrugged.

Thinking he was dismissing her, with a sudden surge of

resentment she silently labelled him a supercilious old pot-head. Although she had to admit it was hard to tell his age. His skin was smooth except for faint crow's-feet at the edge of his eyes. There were creases in his jaw. However old he might be, she thought, he was really quite exotically good-looking.

"One of a kind," he said suddenly. "Hand-made, a long time ago, by my grandfather."

His tone, which was quite gentle, surprised her. His accent, while American, had an unusual quality: the familiar-enough drawl, but somehow rounded, not gritty, the vowels sliding seductively.

As if making an offering, he held the flute out to her on the open palm of his hand.

Moving to take it, Kathy noted his long, lean fingers and broad palm. The skin was paler on the underside of his hand. She wondered how it would feel on her body.

A faint fluttering began in her stomach: a thousand tiny butterflies taking wing. Shocked at the way her thoughts had gone, she hesitated, noting an ostentatious silver ring set with a turquoise stone on the third finger of his left hand. She couldn't tell if it was a signet ring, or a wedding ring.

But why should she care if he was married?

Her ears grew hot. Careful not to touch his hand and struggling to control the sudden shakiness of her own, she picked up the instrument and pretended to examine it, hoping he hadn't noticed. What was the matter with her? He'd think she was in awe of him, like some kind of star-struck groupie. And then he might try and seduce her.

The thought made her go all woozy.

Making herself focus on the flute, she saw there wasn't much to the small, straight, wooden instrument. It was old, and well-worn. A faint image that looked like a dog was carved into it.

"Is this some kind of dog?" Her voice came out as a pathetic strangled imitation of itself. To her dismay, she realised she was being everything she had promised herself she wouldn't be when she got close to one of the upper realms of the film-crew.

"Hrrmph."

It was as if her ears were stuffed with cotton-wool, and it didn't feel right to ask him to repeat the word. At a loss, Kathy frowned. She had to calm her silly reaction. Be cool. A bright penny dropped in the confused recesses of her mind.

"Your playing, it sounded like a wolf. Not howling," she added quickly, "but sort of singing...."

He smiled then, a small smile, but not at her, more to himself, his straight white teeth bright against the tan of his skin, the creases in his jaw and cheek cutting deeply.

"Sometimes I like to be alone, howl at the moon," he said. "An' the sun kinda looks like a moon right now, bein' so pale."

With a strange sort of swoosh, even as she wondered if he was trying to tell her he wanted to be alone, everything clicked into place.

"Oh, my God. You're a red Indian, aren't you?"

The words had popped out of her mouth before she'd thought how it might sound, and seemed to hang in the air, in the little mist formed by her breath. If they had dissipated as easily, it wouldn't have been so bad. She simply hadn't thought of it till that moment, and had blurted it out. Her big mouth, as usual. What if it was rude to call them that? What if he was simply from Mexico? But how could she be expected to know the difference?

He remained still, his eyes narrow, his face expressionless.

Why didn't he answer? Kathy's heart was racing. She was sure she was right, even though she'd never seen one in real life before. No-one would believe her. And how on earth did a red Indian get to be working on a movie?

As if standing outside himself, Joe watched the all too familiar patterning grind into action. Almost he told the girl to take off. Save himself the hassle, as much as her. Yet even as he remembered his promise to himself, he found himself assessing.

Early twenties; easier to tell when there was no make-up. Attractive, although her face was thin, the skin stretched over the bones, and her nose and cheeks were red from the cold. Her mouth looked soft, moist. The clothes they'd given her made her bulky, hiding a body that might be any shape, but youth always looked good. Dressed in a cardboard box, youth would look good. And he'd always had a weakness for tall, pale-eyed blondes. From her accent, she was local. He'd rated the local people as friendly and well-intentioned, if direct. Like the way she'd spoken that, right out; although give her credit for being quick. He found himself taking the next step in a ritual dance he thought he'd put behind him.

"In Dios," he murmured, nodding gently. "You don't need be afraid. I ain't here to scalp you."

That came out like reading a script, he thought. I'm losing my touch. He felt slightly ridiculous, spinning it out yet again and making his voice creamily amused like that, but her reaction fed the old wolf in him.

"Afraid?" Her voice was breathless. "Oh, no. It's just that I've never-"

"Had the pleasure?" Knowing she'd pick up the double-meaning, a better part of him curled up at this kind of subversive toying. He normalised his tone, indicating the fallen tree-trunk beside him. "Visit with me awhiles. I'm gettin' a crick in my neck, looking up at you, English wench."

She hesitated fractionally, eyeing the log as if it were some kind of trap, then did as he asked. He caught a faint, flowery scent; a familiar undertone: her perfume; the smell of the wardrobe trailer.

"Sorry if I offended you," she said hurriedly, hugging her legs. "It just came out and that wasn't very polite. I mean, you're not exactly, like, red. My Mam's always telling me to think before I speak, but I believe it's best to say what's in your mind, you know?"

Thinking how the English were always apologising, Joe looked at the watery sun, waiting with the patient courtesy of his people to see whether she was finished, or just collecting her thoughts. The silence stretched, and he decided to break it.

"Mind's a strange thing, filled with little voices that babble. In between, in the spaces, that's where the important things lie. Things that often can't be spoke. Things of the heart."

In truth, Joe had never given much thought to what might be inside a woman's mind. But he knew what they liked to hear. Peripheral vision informed him that her eyes had widened. His little gem had been suitably enigmatic and poetic, and impressed her. Although he had to admit to himself it had been good, right off the top of his head like that.

"I sort of know what you mean," she said after a few moments. "All the things that worry you can go round and round in your head, going nowhere. Then there's a sunset, or something. And nothing else matters except how beautiful it is, and you remember what's most important. And you can't tell a soul; there's not the words, and no-one would understand, anyway."

Feeling a strange twist in his chest, Joe looked down at his hands. He always worked slowly, giving himself time to think, but her ready understanding threw him a little.

"That beauty...." Purposely, he softened his voice. "The only goal for man is beauty, an' the only beauty is the harmony of nature...." A wide arc of his arm encompassed the trees around them; the unseen land beyond; the world. "Our Holy People taught us originally. It's a simple truth. But it ain't so simple, learnin' to look for the pattern, finding your place in it, an' going in beauty.... A life-long lesson."

He sensed the bait had been taken; the hook was stuck fast. Now to just reel her in. But this time there was no high, just a nauseating awareness of yet another shameful exploitation of his heritage. And this one wouldn't fight, wouldn't even wriggle: a challenge he used to relish.

"That's really beautiful," she said dreamily. But a few moments later, she was back down to earth: "So, where are you from?"

Joe hesitated. Part of him wanted shot of the old self, which had a mind and life of its own. Knowing it wouldn't be what she wanted to hear, he dully replied, "L.A."

"Los Angeles? I wouldn't have thought-"

"That's where the action is."

"Oh, of course. But it must be ... so very different to here. How do you find it?"

Typical sandstorm of confused whiteman mind. Yet Joe was amused, wondering if she was now trying not to be so direct. "Red Indians can get on a plane, too."

"Oh, I didn't mean.... I meant it must be different to be out in the middle of nowhere, in a tiny country like England, after a city like Los Angeles."

He shrugged at the obviousness of it.

"And I have to ask," she added, "are you, like, in a tribe? Do they still have them? And living in wigwams?"

Using their illusions always worked. He'd be gone from here, soon enough. Why not enjoy her while she lived out a little fantasy? Give her something to spice up her small-town life; a story to tell her friends. The tactics were straightforward, like in the military: a mechanical movement of bodies, fuelled by the hunger of his body.

"Sure. 'Less they turned extinct while I been gone." Joe shrugged, knowing the effect the words would have, although they couldn't have been much further from the truth.

"Oh, how awful. I saw a movie once, that one about the last Mohican. How can you stand it?"

Joe shook his head. "All what happened.... The way of the Dineh's always been to adapt, and endure. There's always a pattern...." His tongue felt thick and clumsy, like the words he was using didn't really belong there. Uneasily, he shifted position.

"Dineh?" she asked.

"They call us Navajo." Feeling as if he had given away too much, he needed to move away from the subject. Although he wasn't really interested, he steered her thoughts: "You grow up here?"

The girl scrunched up her face, an oddly-appealing gesture that left white lines imprinted across the bridge of her reddened nose.

"Born and bred. On my Mam's side. Generations of us. We're some of the original border reivers."

Joe was in fact fascinated to hear of her maternal bloodline, one of the clans that had held the borderlands at a time when Northumbria had been a great kingdom in its own right. A buffer between the English and the Scots, like wheat between millstones, they'd been ground down to their essence: a fierce, independent people, living by their own code. He watched her, enjoying how she grew spirited in the telling of ancient feuds, the honour of the clan; things to which he could easily relate. Her pale eyes became stormy-bright, and she punctuated her excited little tale with waves of her hands and stabs of her fingers.

In his mind's eye, a swift and silent raiding party passed though deep forest and over desolate moors, cloaks rippling behind them, the wind singing in their ears. Swarming down on the great hall, hurling themselves upon the sentries: a close, sweaty combat; the immediacy of a life-and-death struggle. He imagined frantically-barking dogs, the grunt and shriek of fighting men and women, their laboured breath steaming, the smell of the smoky tapers and stench of freshly-spilled blood on mud and straw. And, after, exhilarated with their daring and their victory, he'd throw himself on her.

The brief, erotic moment passed like a shadow, making Joe shiver, and he looked up at the wintry sky, as if seeking its source there. His mind had really run away on him that time.

Kathy saw the distant look in his eyes and thought he must have grown bored. "Only now ... it's, like, so totally boring round here. Nothing ever happens."

She realised how pathetic she sounded: like she had no kind of life. Or like she was trying to hint at something. Racking her brain, she realised that this was what she'd dreamed of happening: here she was, sitting on a log of all places, actually talking with a big-wig from the film set. If that's what he was; it didn't feel right to ask. But she'd seen him right at the centre, just before the take. Even if he hadn't been the one to give the cues, he was always with the camera-men and crew, and he talked easily with the cast, and they were famous. Maybe her wish had come true; maybe this was her moment, her chance. Only she didn't know how to move it forward. The ongoing silence began to make her feel uncomfortable.

"You said.... What was your tribe?" she blurted out, embarrassed at not catching it the first time.

"Navajo."

His abruptness chilled her. She nodded, although she was sure he'd given her another name before. Maybe it was rude to ask like this. Yet she couldn't resist: "Umm ... can I ask your name, your own name, I mean?"

"Joe."

She couldn't keep the disappointment out of her voice: "But don't you have a proper Indian name? You know, like they have in 'Dances with Wolves'?"

He didn't reply, didn't even look at her. The silence grew.

Kathy tightened her lips. She could have kicked herself. Why couldn't she keep her mouth shut? How stupid was it to think they still had those poetic names, like in the films. Or maybe it was a private thing. Probably he was only being polite, answering her questions, while he really wanted to be left in peace. She wished she could sit so still and silent. But the damp was seeping through the cheap, rough material of the skirt, and her feet were frozen. Rubbing the chilled skin of her hands, she shifted uneasily.

Yet she couldn't simply get up and leave. Some of the things he had said were still chasing round in her mind: what he'd said about harmony, about beauty. She'd never heard a man talk like that before.

Joe was aware of her face: interesting, open. Despite feeling like an intruder, he could read the emotions running across it, like cloud-shadows across the landscape. But he was not exactly clear in himself. He didn't mind her outspokenness, or a certain strength he could sense; it was natural for him to see woman as equal. Maybe it was the way whiteman asked for a name; they rarely identified themselves first, to a newcomer to the area.

Questioning the wisdom of continuing the game dulled the anticipation; the short time before he sank his teeth into the meat, his mouth fresh and alive with juices, was somehow not the same. And the thought of dancing it all through to another sacrificial ending held him still and undecided. Like storm-clouds gathering on the horizon, a sense of foreboding lurked at the edge of his mind.

Putting it down to tiredness, to the effects of the dope, Joe persuaded himself how easy and pleasurable it would be to fill a couple of nights with this awestruck girl. In return, she'd have a little diversion, a little adventure. And it would be interesting to taste the flavour of this cold and wet little island. Why deprive himself when it was being presented to him on a plate, wrapped up in a pretty little package? He tapped a finger against his breastbone, preparing to reel her in.

"Who knows why the flute called you? Someone, or something, seems to have made sure of our meeting."

Yet even as he observed the effectiveness of his words, he felt torn. Her eyes were wide and shining, like a trapped doe's. For the first time, he was terribly clear about how untrue to himself he was being.

A sudden clattering among the branches above their heads marked the departure of a pair of roosting wood-pigeons, as a figure crashed through the underbrush and emerged into the glade.

"For chrissake, Joe," the broad, black-bearded, down-jacketed young man burst out impatiently, "been lookin' for you near a half-hour. Jess says it pisses him off the way you leave your cell-phone turned off. He wants a pow-wow." Without waiting for a reply, he turned and disappeared swiftly back the way he'd come.

Feeling as if she'd been somehow caught out, Kathy had willed herself invisible. But the crew-member, a go-fer, she imagined, was gone; it was as if she were no more than a prop. Or maybe, she thought uneasily, he was used to seeing Joe with young extras.

Joe stood up, rising with an ease and grace that belied the amount of time he'd been sitting there, cross-legged. Her own legs felt stiff with cold. Then she saw his outstretched hand, silently offering to help her up. Thinking it an unusual, old-fashioned, gentlemanly sort of thing to be doing, and not sure whether she wanted to be touched by him after all, she almost pretended she hadn't seen it.

Totally unprepared for the wild tingling that raced up her arm and down through her body as their skin met, Kathy's felt as if she'd stuck her fingers into an electrical socket. Light-headed, a strange kind of quivering feeling in her belly, her legs soft and weak, she was deeply aware of his hand gripping hers, cool and smooth and strong. It was all she could do to stand up in as normal a way as possible. As he released her hand again, she wondered what on earth had happened; and then whether he had he felt it too. Trembling with the intensity of it, she glanced at him.

Shadowed by the black hat, his face was unreadable. His dark eyes were looking at some place beyond her shoulder.

"But why, I wonder?"

For a long, incredible moment, Kathy thought he must mean the amazing sensation. Then she realised it was as if, to him, there'd been no interruption, none at all: no pigeons leaving, no go-fer sent to summon him. Feeling dizzy again, she had to close her eyes. And while she had no idea what would happen, the next part seemed inevitable.

His hands were light on her upper arms; she barely felt them through the coarse material of the jacket. There was a faint smell of something like damp wool, then a radiating warmth near her face. Every nerve in her body quivering, she held still and waited. The scent of his breath was sweet, like dried grass. Then his lips brushed hers, a feather touch, soft and dry.

Her entire body flooded with the tingling. It coursed hotly up into her neck and face; it made her breasts ache, a sweet ache echoed by the melting, throbbing feeling in her lower belly and thighs. The contact was over in a second, but she wanted him to touch her again; wanted those long, strong hands to stroke the aching places....

Knees weak, she grabbed his sleeves and clung to him like he was the anchor in a storm. He cupped the back of her head in his hand and gently pressed her cheek against the rough wool of his coat. Her head felt cradled; she rode the rise and fall of his chest as he sighed deeply.

Throat tight, jaw aching, unaware of the myriad ways she betrayed herself, Kathy felt nauseous with wanting him. Her body at once soft and rigid and glowing with yearning, she leaned into him, as if pulled by an irresistible force. The strength of her desire shocked and thrilled her. And when she heard the low moan, she barely recognised her own voice.

She thought she'd experienced falling in love, but it was nothing like this.

Joe could feel the girl, like she was vibrating, and knew he could have her that very moment if he wanted. Yet it was a new and strange thing, the way his lips still bore a trace of fire from that purposely-tantalising brush against her lips, as much as the unexpectedly immediate response in his groin.

Reflexively, he sniffed the air. Mouldering decay, all around; a metallic tang, hinting of snow; her warm, salty woman-scent, an undertone to the flowery perfume. His mouth watered. Most likely she was unaware of how she was pressing her body against his; all of her, breast, stomach, thighs; nothing held back....

Something hard was pressing into his back. His flute, still in her hand. The cold air licked at his lips as if they were raw. Her long, faint moan, like a dying animal, resounded in his head.

And in truth, it was not in his blood to interfere with even an animal.

Looking down at the top of the girl's head, at the tangle, the irregular parting, the pale furrow of naked scalp, Joe couldn't work out what was going on inside him. Almost he pushed her away. But the moment passed, and for no reason he could fathom, he found himself feeling sad and protective of her at the same time.

TWO

In the west, the sun is sinking. The light in the clearing is gloomy. Stark, heavy branches, darkened by recent rain, crowd the small patch of deepening sky. Gnarled, twisted and furred with moss, a mesh of exposed roots lies at the foot of the old trees, twining among each other like a gorgon nightmare. The earth is carpeted with ivy, glinting dull-green, threading its way up tree-trunks and along naked branches, giving an illusion of leaves.

His back against a tall and smooth, angular stone, worked to a tapering point as if to indicate a star in the heavens, a moustached man waits. His face is sombre and weary, and his dark hair, hanging loose, glints with threads of silver. An old scar creases his forehead, while another, raised white, mars his cheek and bristled jaw. His scuffed boots are ankle-deep in dry leaves, and his deep-blue cloak, pulled close about his body, is stained and torn. One gloved hand is on the hilt of the sword protruding from the folds of the cloak, as if he anticipates attack; the other is clenched in a fist by his side.

A wind is rising. It sneaks around the glade, lifts the man's hair and ruffles the edge of his cloak. Seeming to lose heart as it provokes no response, it ascends, seeking solace among the sleeping trees.

The underbrush quivers and parts. A bent, cloaked figure emerges from the tangle of twig and thorn, and steps up to the man, who remains as if carved from stone.

Pushing back his hood, the new-comer reveals a fleshy skull, wispy white hair, faded rheumy eyes, parchment skin.

"You said my name." His voice is a hoarse rasp. "When you name something, you call it."

The waiting man glances uneasily at the trees. "Yes. Of course. But how do I know a name is true?" His words mist the still, cold air.

The old man shrugs. "Who knows the true name?"

"If I did, I wouldn't need you."

Man and mage stare at each other, creating a tension that is almost palpable. It is as if they are about to engage arms: thrust of staff meeting cut of sword. But neither moves. Minutes pass.

Finally, Merlin straightens. He thrusts his staff against the ground, as if seeking the power of the earth. He speaks clearly, his voice a strong, ringing tone: "I have been here, many times, ignored. You have been near me, Lancelot, many times, but your mind is deep and dense as the wood, and you miss me. Each time, you pass me by. You are not in this wood alone. And remember, when you summon good, the shadow always rides with it."

Lancelot tenses and looks over his shoulder at the tall, black trees. Great sentinels, they might have been guarding the small space since time began. When the knight looks back, the old enchanter is gone.

Shivering like a stranded jellyfish, Kathy knew it was not just from the rising, cold east wind. All day she had tried to work out what it was about Joe that made him stand out; she thought he looked wonderful, better even than she remembered, although they'd only met the day before. She loved the black tendril of his pony-tail curled over the back of his collar; his cool black hat and long coat; his intensity; his strange stillness. She'd tried to keep an eye on him for most of the day, and watched how he would have a few words with just about every member of the crew, as well as the actors, before they'd start shooting.

If only, she wished, he'd done that with the extras, too. This time, ages had been spent over the lights, and there seemed to have been a few tests with the audio equipment. Then they'd got going for real. She even found it exciting to watch other people doing as he indicated.

Her eyes followed the tall, upright figure in the long black coat as he went over to speak to the old actor, white-haired Robinson.

Her excitement beginning to give way to panic, with all her heart and for what she thought had to be the hundredth time that day, Kathy willed Joe to look her way. This was the final scene; now they'd be wrapping up. She had to do something; today was the last day they needed extras. This was her last chance.

She hadn't imagined things would be so difficult; that the chance to be seen by him, to speak to him again, so elusive. As soon as they'd got there (not early enough for her, this time), she'd rushed to find out when they'd be needed and to her delight, had been told to wait until called; this time a loudspeaker would be giving the extras their cue to dress.

It had seemed like a sign; dragging a reluctant Emily along so she wouldn't seem too obvious, she'd scouted round the trailers and the other vehicles but hadn't been able to find Joe anywhere by the time they'd been called. It had been maddening; she'd worn her black leather jacket, her favourite sea-green velour jumper which brought out the faint flecks of green in her eyes, the thick green-grey knitted scarf which she knew looked good, wrapped round her neck twice, her skinny black jeans and her silver-and-malachite hoop earrings.

Then she'd had to put up with the wardrobe-girls, telling her off as if she were a child, making her scrub off the make-up that had taken ages to get right and messing up and spraying her freshly-washed hair so it looked matted and dirty again.

But at least she'd found out that Joe was one of the top brass, who'd all gone off to inspect another location.

Everything seemed so disorganised. This time it was the crew as well as the extras who had to hang round half of the morning, getting paid for doing nothing, until two vehicles came roaring up. Her heart had leapt and thrummed in her throat when she recognised Joe, and she'd made a note of the vehicle he'd been driving.

But there hadn't been a single chance to get near him the entire day. She couldn't find the courage to approach him; then she'd had to wait ages to slowly gather a bundle of firewood and tie it up and carry it away over her shoulder – four times – in the background of a long take with Guinevere and Lancelot that she could make no sense of, being too far away to catch any of the words. In another, she'd had to simply walk along a muddy track between the trees with Emily and several anonymous others, including the irritating local lad, to scramble out of the way when a group of horsemen thundered by. Three takes, for no reason she could work out other than the riders had needed to race faster and look more menacing.

The ugly shoes she'd been given to wear again had leaked; her feet were wet and freezing.

Now she could only watch from a distance as Joe walked towards the trailers with the old actor, the one who played Merlin. She chewed her lip in frustration. Emily had gone to the catering coach with the others for sandwiches and tea, but food was the last thing on Kathy's mind. Rubbing her chilled hands, she hurried to the marquee where the clothes were kept.

Swiftly changing back into her own clothes, Kathy kept repeating one name under her breath, over and over, not even stopping when she looked uselessly for a mirror so she could repair her hair and her make-up. In the end, she had to do it without one. By the time she got back outside, the heavy, grey clouds that had been threatening from the east had finally trailed in and a thick drizzle was sweeping through the site. At a loss, she wandered over to the transport vehicles and began to look for a dark-green jeep.

Her body burred and jangled; she had barely slept and hadn't been able to eat all day.

She had no idea what she might do. The day before, on the coach home, she'd found out from the driver that the entire film-crew were staying at the Percy Arms, in town. But she couldn't imagine doing what she'd done last night again.

Instead of going to the pub with the usual crowd, she'd surprised her Mam by taking Trixie out for a long walk. Which of course had happened to take her, several times, past the Percy. But she hadn't bumped into him, coming out or going in, no matter how much she willed it. Not even when she'd plucked up the courage to go into the bar. By the time they'd chased her out, telling her she should know better than to come in with a dog, she'd still seen no sign of anybody connected to the film. After all the possible scenarios that had passed through her mind, to realise she'd drawn a big blank had almost made her ill.

Berating herself for not giving him her phone number at the time – although she didn't know how she could have, there hadn't been a chance – she'd lain awake almost the whole night, going over and over the precious memory: the strange music; the intriguing accent; the way he sat on the bare ground as if it wasn't the middle of winter; how he'd shown her his flute; the feel of his hands on her arms....

Unsure if she'd slept at all, she'd been up at five so she could get properly ready, and had been first in the queue for the mini-bus at the market-place, in a kind of feverish trance. Emily had guessed something was going on, but Kathy found she couldn't tell her a thing. Emily would laugh, make stupid jokes; even worse, tell the others. And the whole thing would be spoiled.

Even now, she could hardly believe it herself. How could she tell anyone that his words had been like poetry to her ears? She had always loved poetry, something which she'd had to keep secret, because she knew she would have been royally mocked, both at school and at home. And he was wise. Some of the things he'd said had seemed to open up places in her mind she'd never been to before.

For as long as she could remember, she'd had this powerful

feeling about The One, the one and only, meant to be. When she was nine or ten, falling asleep at night, she'd used to entwine her hands on the pillow by her face and imagine she was holding The One's hand. He'd be mirroring her position, looking deep into her eyes, as loving, fulfilled and content as she. It had never been sexual, not even when she got interested in that side of things; it had somehow been beyond that: a peaceful imagining-longing that she was sure would come true, one day. And despite everyone laughing at her for believing in fairy-tales, she'd hung onto her dream, learning to keep it close to herself, a secret jewel that she took out less and less as time passed by and her innocence was hardened by experience.

And this was it; she knew it. It was light-years beyond anything she'd ever known. Billy, back in school, had been an immature crush compared to this. As for Tim, after the first couple of weeks, she had hardly missed him when he went off to university. Seeing him in the holidays had been more from habit than anything, and although the sex was fun, they didn't have that much in common, especially since he had begun a whole new life working in Leeds.

Joe and Kathy. Joseph and Katherine. Like royalty, she thought, running the two names together in an unceasing round in her head. She couldn't care less that he was older, and thought she'd never get over the fact that The One should've turned out to be a handsome red Indian who talked so poetically and romantically. And of all people, she realised, she had the old crow, Blackie, to thank. If the bank manager hadn't told her about the ad in the Gazette, she'd have missed this opportunity.

For the umpteenth time, Kathy thought back to the magical flute meeting. For in her mind, that's what it had become. Although she couldn't remember much about it and had only been an usher, she recalled enjoying Mozart's opera, performed in her final year at school as a special fund-raising event.

Licking her lips, she relived the feather-touch of his, and fantasised about what might have happened next, if only they hadn't been interrupted. Then she recalled how she'd moaned when he had held her, and felt her face go hot at the memory. It had been so embarrassing. But she hadn't been able to help it.

Any more than she couldn't help but be in this pathetic situation of hanging round empty vehicles in a muddy field in freezing rain. There was only these two days' work.

Close to despair, Kathy knew this was her last chance.

The final straw had been having to wait for the low-flying jets to finish their exercise. Another thing that should have been checked out in advance. Although it had worked out: because they'd run late, the thickening gloom in the last shot had made it all the more effective.

"Cut you into a game of poker tonight."

He knew Melanie was trying to include him, not understanding his need.

"Jesus, Joe," she said in annoyance when he didn't respond. "You're such an unsociable prick. When I think of all the casinos you people run.... Only joking; some of my best friends are.... Come on, at least come and have dinner with us." She tugged at his arm.

Joe didn't like being touched in this way. He knew it as a weakness, but still he stiffened. Melanie didn't seem to notice. Or if she did, she wasn't giving up yet.

"What d'you get up to in your room, on your own? High times, eh?" she added provocatively, giving his arm a squeeze. "Don't you get kinda lonely?"

Knowing her situation and having met her husband, Joe knew this was not a proposition. But how to explain he never felt loneliness? Why explain? It was simple: he always looked forward to time alone. And now, especially. It didn't come easy, working with some of these people; he needed to renew his spirit. But none of this would mean anything to whiteman, as afraid of being alone as he was of the dark; always having to fill in the spaces, never seeming to realise the fullness of silence. It was a blessing that the winter days were short.

He shrugged, but made an offering: "I'm tired."

"I know it's been a lousy day," Melanie said placatingly. "Jess and his not-thought-through ideas, wasting time like that. Then the camera...."

"And Owen, losin' his cool," Joe recalled. "Hah! Openly flourishing his flask an' gettin' loaded. Not that it slows him down any."

"It's not him. I can see you get on with Owen; better than anyone else here, in fact.... Just don't let Jess get to you."

"It's always people. Camera can be fixed, but once a person got somethin' whirrin' round in their pea-brain...." Unable to resist, Joe mimicked Jess's drawl: " 'I like that, keep goin' on that track. You were really in his head then. Put it in the pot; let it simmer.' "

Melanie laughed. "You should be on the other side of the lens."

Joe felt bad. It wasn't right to mock or criticise a person behind his back. A lightning-flash struck, somewhere far behind his eyes.

"You know where we are if you change your mind," she added.

Watching her walk away, Joe reflected on what she'd dubbed "the battle of wills". His view of the movie as a vehicle to transport people beyond the mundane reality of daily life, to remind them of what it is to have a vision, seemed set against those who saw it as just another quasi-historical soap, a money-spinner.

Yet he'd been head-hunted for this job. Someone had believed in him, in whatever it was they thought he could bring to one of the great myths of a faraway, cold little island.

Joe had always been fascinated by mystery. And to him, life was the greatest mystery of all. He thought about how the pattern of his own life had been lost to him for a long, dark time. And in that time, his mind forgot that ugliness was of its own creation. It had been a hard journey, back to that simple truth.

Approaching the memory cautiously, instinctively careful to contain the anger, he remembered going back, trying to explain. But most of his relatives had laughed at his dream. Yet he'd not only come through the whiteman's education system, but was gaining recognition in the arena that had called him, so late in life.

It was not about the money; he had seen how no-one got rich without cheating others. Nor was it about his name being attached to it; it was not the owning of the thing that absorbed him, but its creation. It was fulfilling something of the story-teller in him, a twentieth-century story-teller. It was about touching hearts and minds with a great truth, and with a sense of the supernatural.

He had never spoken of it, but appreciated how his racial heritage, which had seemed to have come at enormous cost, also came with a great reward. Not only the life-way, but the land. The immense, arid, eroded, dramatic wilderness of his blood and bones, with its garish sunsets and sandblasted stone sculptures, had shaped his soul.

Something of it was echoed here, he knew, in this vacant, gloomy landscape, where the bones of the land were laid bare, where the great, open, low-bellied sky scraped hills rounded and softened by millions of years of exposure, and draped the land with dark clouds like a blanket.

Another flash of light flickered at the edge of his vision. Aware of the immanence of a migraine, like an approaching thundercloud, Joe headed over to his vehicle. Under the wan internal light, he rummaged in his carry-all. Instead of the little vial of pills, however, his fingertips encountered the soft plastic wrapping of his stash.

Maybe, he thought, this was a sign to give the tablets a miss, roll a joint and drive awhile. Picking up the book he'd left lying on the seat, one of the many Owen had loaned him, he noticed it was the one was about Guinevere. The cover was entrancing. Her shining red-gold hair was braided and coiled about her head, her skin pale and flawless. Her long cloak, deep, velvety green-blue and embellished with golden crescents and stars and pinned at the shoulder with a massive, tri-spiral silver brooch, was draped about her slim shoulders and fell heavily to the ground. Of the same colour, her dress was edged at neck and wrist with a gold embroidered pattern. Wrapped round her narrow waist was a wide, intricately-woven leather girdle, and at her throat gleamed a slender silver torc. In one hand, she was holding a massive old iron key.

A noble and beautiful queen, played by the beautiful Julia Noble. Everyone still laughed about that, but it touched him, somehow.

A faint, cool prickling trickled down Joe's spine, informing him of a presence behind him.

Kathy hesitated. He had appeared so suddenly, and didn't seem to have noticed her. But then she had been round the back of the vehicle.

It wasn't going at all like she'd imagined, not one of the many permutations that had filled her sleepless night or this long, increasingly disappointing day. And now, in the semi-darkness, a drizzling, cold rain sweeping across her hot face, she felt small and self-conscious, approaching him as he was about to get into his vehicle and drive away, clearly without any thought of her in his head.

"Hi, Joe," she said, the shakiness of her voice echoing the trembling in her stomach. "Um, we met yesterday, remember? In the woods? Your Pied Piper trick?" Shifting her feet, she gave an embarrassed laugh, her face growing even hotter as she realised how her last words might be taken.

With the car-light behind him, she couldn't see his face. A faint aroma, earthy and musky with a hint of cannabis, drifted her way, and her inner trembling intensified.

"Yeah, right."

The slight huskiness, the drawling intonation ... she recognised his voice as everything she remembered and more, but his tone seemed horribly cool. Surely he remembered what had happened, she thought desperately. He was the one who'd said that something special had brought them together, confirming what she'd felt, even before she knew it. She had no idea what to say next. The silence stretched and stretched, until she thought she'd break apart.

"I don't think I told you my name. It's Kathy." The normality of telling him her name felt something of a let-down. "Um, yesterday, I looked out for you, after. But we had to leave before you were done. And today ... well, I had to wait till now for an opportunity to speak to you. They don't need us after today, you see. And now, I've missed the bus back...." Realising how pathetic she sounded, as if she might have planned it this way, she stopped, wishing she could see his face.

"Guess I didn't notice you. Don't take it personal. Good extras create atmosphere, add to the reality. They don't take the limelight."

"Fat chance of that, looking like I did." Self-consciously, Kathy pushed at her hair with stiff, cold fingers. It was matted with hairspray, sticky and wet.

He said nothing.

Kathy wondered if he had heard her. She could hardly believe how he was being; it was as if he barely remembered her and couldn't care less. Maybe, she thought, he gets pestered by women all the time and this is how he gets rid of them. Her heart sank. Then she remembered that he'd been the one who'd said how they had met was special.

"Well, now," he said neutrally, after what seemed like another age. "I'm headin' back into town. Guess you could use a ride?"

"Please." She nodded, relief flooding her body, yet scarcely able to believe in the ordinariness of it all. She began to think that she must have made more of it than had really been the case. It was hard to remember now, with everything that had gone on in her mind, since. Something inside her began to cool, to darken.

Joe was silent until they reached the road.

"Kathy."

Surprised and pleased, Kathy looked at him. He was shifting gear, his eyes on the road. She waited for him to continue, and when he didn't, realised he might not have known he'd said it. People sometimes did that: spoke out loud what was in their mind without realising they'd done it. She wondered if he had been repeating her name to himself in his mind, so he'd remember it. Whatever it was about, he had to have been thinking about her for it to sort of leak out like that. And it had sounded wonderful, the personal nature of it carried on the rolling timbre of his voice, somehow deeply intimate.

Her name seemed to haunt the car's interior like a dark bird. Surreptitiously, she watched his profile, drinking it in: the gleam of reflected light in his eye; the sleek, black hair; the distinctive nose; the silhouetted pursing curve of his lips.

A delicious, swoony, melting feeling resumed in her stomach. She wanted to reach across the gear-stick, touch his thigh. Get things moving, or at least make things clear. But another part of her held her back, wishing that the moment, the ride would simply last and last; that they could be like this forever, with him in the driver's seat. She looked away, feeling stupid, like a star-struck teenager.

Through a shadowy, bristling gauntlet of hedgerows they passed, headlights silvering the misting drizzle. Only when they were approaching the outskirts of town did he speak again.

"So, where d'you want I should drop you off?"

For a few seconds, Kathy's mind refused to work.

"Market-place'll do," she said dully.

All her wonderful feelings took a nose-dive. Was that it? A ride into town? All she could think was that she didn't want to get out of this distinctive vehicle anywhere near her house. She couldn't bear the thought of anyone seeing her being dumped, which was how it felt. What had gone wrong? Was it how she looked? But he hadn't seemed to care, before.

It was all slipping away, like a dream. She felt like wailing. Instead, locked into a frozen state, she tightly gripped the car-seat and stared out blindly into the night.

So unseeing was she, that she barely noticed he'd driven past the market-place. Then she almost said something, but it wasn't as if it were invisible: the market cross jutted up in plain view. At the Percy Arms, he parked close to the entrance, turned off the engine and sat quietly, staring ahead, his hands crossed over the wheel.

Why had he brought her here? The throbbing in her throat resumed, and the millions of butterflies were back, deep in her belly. Somehow, Kathy knew she was at a crossroad. And she still had a choice: get out and walk away, be home in ten minutes, clean herself up and go to the pub, have a giggle with Ems about her narrow escape and game of pool later with one of the lads. And back to work tomorrow, safe and sound. Round and round....

The other option yawned before her like a great, dark mouth about to swallow her up. "There be dragonnes," like it said on the ancient maps, when they thought they'd reached the edge of the world. The tension in the car felt so thick she could barely breathe.

There wasn't any choice; not really.

"At your service, marm." Joe had made his voice sound gritty and drawling, like a cowboy's in the movies. She had the feeling she ought to know who it was, and supposed he was trying to make her laugh. But she also knew that he was saying it was up to her now; she had to be the one to make the decision.

But he seemed so distant. And what if she were wrong?

"There was a Joe in my class at school," she began, wondering where she was going with herself. "My granddad, he was friends with this Joe's granddad, all his life. And he was always angling to get me together with him, 'cause they were a big farming family. Gentleman farmers. They had a lot of land, in the family for centuries, and they were really well-off, they used to have ever so many farm-workers and didn't have to do any of the hard work themselves.... I knew Granddad only wanted what was best for me. But I was never one to do what I was told....

"Well, anyway, that Joe was a wild one. Only sixteen when he got a girl pregnant...." Kathy felt her face grew hot and bit her lip. She had no idea what had got into her, and knew she was making a total fool of herself.

Uncharacteristically, Joe took his time in the shower. Not wasting water was a deeply-ingrained habit, but he let the water fall over him, as if it might sluice away the storm-cloud that threatened in the distance. He wished he'd had that toke. And he was tired.

Days that began badly tended to end badly. What had he been thinking of, bringing her back here? He needed to be on his own, get a little high happening, and if that didn't work, use the pills to knock himself into oblivion. The girl would be waiting for more flowery lines, the big seduction, a night of passion with a red Indian. A feather in her cap to tell her little friends about.

He thought about the way she tended to rattle. Whiteman neglected to teach his children the value of quiet, of silence. But then they had scared away the animals long ago, and destroyed what remained.

Why speak of such private things? Yet there had been affection underlying the little tale of her grandfather. Trawling in the depths of his own memory, Joe came across a grizzled, white-haired elder, partial to sunglasses, with whose image came the old stories. A dark, indefinable shape tugged at the net, and his mind shied away from the area like a spooked horse.

Irritated, he decided he'd simply offer the girl a meal out, then drop her at her home. That would give her enough to crow about. She was too young. Although that wouldn't have bothered him in the slightest, once. But now that he thought about it, he realised she had to be about Evie's age.

How would he feel about a man his age seducing his daughter? Any man, come to think of it?

A sense of futility was all he could muster. It was hard to rouse much feeling about someone he hadn't seen for near fifteen years. He wondered if she had grown to fit the thick, gleaming fall of black hair that Lindy had fought to tame, blaming him all the while.

Lindy.

Another flash in his head knocked his thoughts awry. When it faded, he realised he couldn't really recall what she looked like any more, except for her long legs, her tawny mane of hair. And now, yet another blonde was waiting for him on the other side of the door.

Why do this thing? Once, he wouldn't have thought twice about it: spinning out the illusion and winning the woman over, knowing he could go on shafting all night. But the lack of any resolution, any kind of peace at all, he knew all that too well.

Chasing emptiness.

He remembered his promise to himself that he wouldn't wear this hat any more. It was his own fault she was here; his own fault the way she'd come chasing after him. Worse than anything whiteman did, the way he misused his heritage.

Turning off the hot water, Joe braced himself. As the cold water hit, he closed his eyes, clenched his fists and tightened the muscles in his upper body.

Darkness; cold. These were real. This, he reminded himself, was what had moved in him for so long he had forgotten who he really was. Anger. Addictions. The long road back. And as soon as yet another temptation, another distraction, raised its pretty little head, he succumbed yet again.

But of course, temptation wouldn't come ugly. He thought of the girl's youth, her lack of experience. They'd have nothing in common. After, he'd feel emptier than ever. It was truer to be simply alone.

His body had adapted to the cold water. Flexing the muscles in his back and chest, Joe tipped his head from one side to the other, forward and back, until the muscles in his neck began to grow warm.

With any luck, he thought, he'd taken so long the girl had given up and left. Wiser to run off this mood, than screw or smoke it off.

As he dried himself, he looked in the mirror. Pulling himself erect, he took a gentle pleasure in his raw-boned look, a return to form. Since taking to the pavements in New York, he'd found it to be another helper. Jay's idea. The running had become something of an addiction, but at least a positive one. And he'd been clear about not pumping away in a gym among narcissistic whiteman fleshpots.

Jay.

A curl of anger licked at his guts. She still lived in him. Could still get to him, after all this time. Time ... not such a great healer after all.

Kathy's hands felt cold and clammy. She needed a drink, but there didn't seem to be any of the little bottles that were always in the little fridge in a room like this, and she should know: she'd used to nick them from the store-room when she'd worked here as a chambermaid in the school summer-holidays. She wondered if she dared call room-service, but it had been bad enough following him past reception, even though she didn't know the woman behind the desk. Although she didn't know why she should care who knew she was here.

She thought about how he hadn't had the decency to offer her something, instead of just disappearing into the ensuite without a word. And he'd been gone an age. The longest shower, water splashing the whole time. She'd rather they had stumbled into the room, pulling each other's clothes off, leaving a trail of them up to the bed....

Unable to sit down, and acutely aware of the king-sized bed dominating the room, pristine sheets neatly folded back, she wondered if it might be for the best if she left before he came back out.

But she couldn't bring herself to do that, either.

She tried the telly, but quickly turned it off again, glad the sound was muted. Not only was it a stupid soap, the most unromantic thing she could imagine at this moment, but it was her Mam's favourite. She'd be watching it, and probably wondering where her daughter was. She momentarily thought about giving her a quick ring to tell her she was staying over at Em's, so she wouldn't worry, then changed her mind. She didn't want him to come out of the bathroom and catch her phoning her mother. She really didn't want to talk to anyone. And it wasn't like she was a kid.

Going over to the dressing-table, Kathy tried to brush her hair out, but it was so matted by hairspray that it hurt too much. It needed washing. Staring at herself in the mirror, she hated what she saw: hair practically in dreadlocks, cheeks and forehead shiny, skin

pale but for two strange red blotches either side of her jaw, like an
allergic reaction.

It wasn't at all how she'd imagined. She wished she had the guts
to simply take off her clothes and join him in the shower. Now, he'd
be bound to take one look at her when he came back out, and send
her home. Then she had a daring thought: not if she'd already taken
all her clothes off and got into bed.

But it hadn't been in her fantasy, being like that.

A pile of books on the long, low table at the foot of the bed
caught her attention. Bending over them, Kathy read: "English
Folk-Heroes"; "The Winter King"; "The Quest of Merlin"; "The
Coming of the King". A fat, dog-eared, leather-bound volume of
Malory's "Le Morte D'Arthur" lay open and she picked up,
remembering her English teacher's love of the book. It seemed
really weird that an American Indian should be interested in ancient
British legends.

Leafing through sheaves of papers beside them, she realised one
of them was a copy of the treatment. There was also a script. Both
were creased, scribbled over everywhere and streaked yellow with
highlighter. She scanned several pages, looking for Arthur's part,
which had seemed curiously lacking. Putting them down none the
wiser, she opened the Filofax she found underneath. Feeling a
twinge of guilt, she read a few lines of Joe's looping, curved
handwriting. Looking sort of old-fashioned, it rambled across the
pages, seeming to be little more than appointments and notes.
There was nothing personal that she could find.

Going to the wardrobe, she pulled open the door. Every item of
clothing was black, except for a carmine-red satin shirt, shocking
as a poppy at a funeral.

Hearing a noise at the bathroom door, Kathy rushed to pick up
one of the books just as Joe came back into the room, wearing a
thick, cream-coloured bathrobe that came down below his knees
and was tied at the waist.

Longer than she'd expected, his hair hung black and wet in
loose, curling tendrils over his shoulders. His calves were smooth,

hairless; his feet wide, solid.

It was a strangely intimate moment. As if they'd been together for years, he unselfconsciously padded barefoot across the room, opened the little fridge, took out a bottle of mineral water and drank half of it down without taking a breath, head tipped back, hair a snaking, dripping black cascade down his back.

Kathy felt odd, breathless. He seemed to be sort of glowing. More than anything she wanted to touch the smooth, pale skin of his throat. Her own skin felt like it was burning and her body quivered in a warm and melting rush, straining to cross the few feet between them. Yet she felt rooted to the floor.

"Intriguin', complex woman, your Guinevere." Joe indicated the book the girl was holding. The luxury of water always restored him: the tension had receded. "Been trackin' her. Owen, the old guy that plays Merlin, he took me where she was born. She was born to a northern clan. Picts."

He silently recalled the narrow winding roads, startled blackface sheep, tough and wiry plant-life. The beauty of scattered colour: violet, rust, yellow, grey, and the endless green. Gentle to the eye; beauty in the bleakness. Age and exposure to such harsh elements had brought to it something of the feminine. Never would he forget the hills the local people liked to call mountains, rounded like the soft breasts of a woman; the clefts where the waters ran, secret, hidden by greenery; and the rain: gentle, female. Strange, how it had stirred him.

A land where elements battled each other like supernatural forces. A big grey sky melding into a moody sea, cold as iron, that nibbled with jagged white teeth the exposed, broken edges of the land; the gusting east wind that crooked the scrubby trees and whipped white the waters. And rain, always the rain, hazing land and sea, erasing the horizon.

The North Sea, he remembered. Name as cold as its truth.

"But what about Arthur?" she cut in across his thoughts. "I

didn't see anybody playing him, and he was the king. What exactly's the film about, anyway?"

She looked even younger, and vulnerable with her hair all mussed up. As she took a deep breath, he was aware of the gentle lift of her breasts: small, as he liked. From the shape and movement of them, he guessed she wasn't wearing anything under her sweater. Which was green, almost the same green as the cloak the queen was wearing on the book-cover he had held as the girl had appeared from the gathering dark.

"Yeah, well...." Joe let his eyes slide down her body to her legs. "There's enough movies on that subject already, I reckon. This's after the battle where the king died. When Guinevere tried to take power, then what happened after, with her and the knight, Lancelot. Not many seem to know she came from the north. An' Lancelot, he had a seat in this area; a castle.... An' that's the way this is bein' played out." Distracted by her physicality, he knew he wasn't being clear but didn't care.

"Oh, that's why it's called 'Northern Lights'.... How much longer have you to go?"

"Almost done. These're the last location shots, these one here in the north. An' all the studio takes have been done, down in London."

The girl bit her lower lip, a habit he'd already noted.

She had a good body, a type he liked: slim, and long thighs. Knowing what he could do to it, and to her, with his prowess and potency, almost made him reconsider. Then he reminded himself: without his own release, it would be just another meaningless performance. He wondered if the heightened colour in her cheeks was simply from being out in the cold all day, or if, coupled with her awkwardness, it might cover her own second thoughts.

If she wanted to leave, he wouldn't argue.

"Look, maybe you'd like to clean up. There's clean towels in there," he indicated the bathroom. "We'll grab a bite to eat, an' I'll run you home."

The girl was looking down at the book in her hand, and didn't respond. He could tell she wasn't really seeing the pages, so he waited. Letting time pass without strain was part of his make-up. When he had learned how it made whiteman nervous, it had become something of a game.

"Is that it?" She tugged at her hair, her voice tremulous.

Joe threw apart his hands, as if letting go a small bird, and saw her lips tighten. For a few moments she was very still, then, looking at the floor, almost imperceptibly she gave a little shake of her head and whispered: "I'll stay here tonight, with you."

Instinctively, he looked away from her face; her candid offer of herself took his breath away. For a split second he was balanced on a knife-edge, then something in him moved: a sense of something approaching, from within. Not the flashes or the pressure, but a dizzying rushing feeling which threatened to suck him up like a little fish in a whirlpool.

He couldn't stop himself. In one smooth, thoughtless stride, he covered the space between them, reached out and took hold of her wrist and pulled her to him. Her skin was cold; the fragile tendons beneath his fingers yielded, and heat sparked in his loins. She looked up at him, her pupils large and dark, her expression both yearning and pained, as if she were fighting an inner battle, and losing. He heard her sigh, knew it for the moment of conquest and almost pushed her away.

Except he couldn't. Irresistible, a powerful floodtide was rising relentlessly from deep within. It was as if his body had been a wintry kingdom, like this land he was passing time in, and suddenly spring was struggling in a frenzy to reach the surface. For a desperate drowning moment, he tried to block it, but then the cold fingers of her other hand touched the skin of his throat, feather-light, electric, and slid inside the collar of his robe.

His lower body surged fire in response to her icy touch, and as she brazenly pushed back his robe, exposing his chest and pressing herself against him, he knew she would feel him, trapped and straining for her. Seemingly of its own accord, his other hand touched and pressed her cheek, downy-soft and warm: the perfect skin of youth. He cupped in his palm her chin, small and rounded like a fruit, closing his eyes because of the sensations, not just at his groin, but in his gut, and the unaccustomed dizziness. He didn't need to take time to build up the layers of anticipation and desire; he wanted her, now, wanted her with a knee-buckling fierceness that shocked him.

"I am the storm; you are the rainbow," he murmured, barely knowing where the words were coming from.

The young couple are pressing her to take care of their little girl. They seem desperate. Their clothes, while once good quality, are tired and scruffy. The young man is wearing a dark-green corduroy jacket with a pale jumper underneath. His hair is carrot-coloured, and tied back in a ponytail; the woman's is dark and straggly. Both of them are good-looking, but they are a bit grubby and seem tired, as if they have had no time to wash or rest.

They tell her it's only for a little while. Kathy has a feeling they are on the run for some reason. Before she can find the words to refuse, they have gone. She has no choice but to take the child home. While she is a sweet and precocious little thing, and very pretty, with bubbly blonde hair, blue eyes and rosy cheeks, Kathy is concerned. She doesn't have the time and feels it shouldn't be her responsibility.

Even though she must only be three or four years old, the child is talking like an adult, but Kathy can barely grasp what she is saying.

They are in the bathroom; the child has had a bath and is wrapped in a white towel. There is water all over the floor. The tiles on the wall are beginning to come away; brown around their edges, they are buckling and peeling off. To Kathy's horror, she sees there are water-stains all along the top of the walls and on the ceiling, and watches in horror as water begins to drip, then run down the walls. The room is about to cave in.

They rush to another room. It is like a living-room, only it is big and barn-like. There are gaping holes in the ceiling, which could be the roof, as she can see sky through the holes. Water is streaming down the walls here, too.

Kathy is appalled and frightened; the whole place falling to pieces around her. She can't believe she never noticed how run-down it was before, and just wants to get out. She doesn't know what to do with the child; somehow it is all her fault.

Kathy picks the little girl up, stuffs her into a cupboard and closes the door. It locks shut. She is horrified by what she is doing since she knows this will probably kill such a small child, and then she will be wanted for murder. But she doesn't know what else to do. Strangely, she feels a sense of relief, and has a feeling that people will understand.

Kathy burst out of the terrible dream. For a long moment, she was completely lost. The strange room she was in, lit by a lamp, might have been part of the dream; then it all came back in a rush and her stomach did a flip. She was alone. Snaking under the rumpled sheets and across the bed, her fingers found a faint trace of warmth.

She sat up, her heart pounding. The baleful red light of the bedside clock read six. The ensuite door was open, but it was dark inside. She remembered the faint noise in her dream, and realised it must have been the door to the room.

He was gone.

Feeling sick, she huddled the duvet around her shoulders. After a night like that, she thought angrily, how could he just leave? And where would he go, when it was still dark outside? And why such a nightmarish dream, after the most amazing night of her life? She would never murder anyone; she couldn't even squash a spider. The images were already fading: the young man with the pony-tail, quite good-looking; the woman already a blur. They had been no-one she knew, nor the child.

A glint on the pillow beside her caught her eye. It was the strange pendant he'd been wearing, much as a tie might be worn. She picked it up. Surprised by the weight of it, she saw it was the head of a bird, carved to look as if it were just emerging from the disc of heavy, shining black stone. The eye was beady bright; the beak, long and cruel. The stone was set in silver and hung on a loop of braided black leather, the ends of which were finished off with silver cones engraved in a spiral design. It was beautiful, in a disturbing kind of way.

It couldn't have been dropped there by accident, she realised; he must have had to go out for some reason and rather than wake her, he'd left her this special, personal thing. Everything was fine, after all.

Although she would have vastly preferred to wake up next to him, Kathy felt an enormous sense of relief. Looping it over her head, she lay back down and closed her eyes.

She could feel the black stone, resting heavy and cold between her breasts. The dream faded, was forgotten, as she ran her hands down over her belly, hips and thighs. Her body felt soft, sated; her skin amazingly silky, and super-sensitive. She remembered how he'd wanted the light left on. He hadn't been reserved at all; just slipped off the robe and stood there totally naked, even though she was still dressed. And she'd been unable to move, even when confronted with his obvious desire for her.

Reviving the memory of the smooth contours of his strong shoulders, his lightly-muscled chest, she went through it all again: the way his long black hair had shadowed his face as he'd undressed her. No-one had ever done that to her before, nor had she ever been kissed like that: so gently, so expressively, and for so long. And he'd found places which she'd never known might be sexy: like the vein on the side of her throat, which he'd examined and stroked so lightly, like he was in awe of it. It had made her so dizzy she had almost collapsed.

Even now, touching it herself, the sensation came back. She remembered how she'd felt him, hard and long against her thigh, and recalled there coming a time, even though he made no move in that direction, when she couldn't wait any longer. Pushing him onto his back, she'd sat astride him, looking down onto his dark, sculpted body, using her fingers to comb the incredible liquidsilkiness of his hair.

She'd always liked sex, but this was miles different to anything she'd experienced. He'd not poked at her at all that whole time, even though he'd been ready, but had let her choose the moment. And what followed had been nothing like what she'd done before: none of the pounding and thrusting and bouncing which often made her feel a little ridiculous. He hadn't done any of that, and he'd stopped her from doing it by holding her hips and making her take him so slowly, she'd been gasping for breath and moaning with the incredible feeling.

And then, when he was deep in her, he'd kept so still it had almost driven her crazy; but he'd held her and himself absolutely still for what seemed like an age, until she'd felt a new sensation growing in her, sort of like when the tide is coming in, the waves getting closer and closer. It had made her want to go wild; to forget herself and crash onto him and drown in him.

She remembered him being over her, and the strange little noises he'd made against her ear, sort of like when you encourage a horse, only softly. It seemed silly now, but at the time it had sounded so sexy she'd almost passed out. Sometime in the middle of it all, they'd fallen asleep, then woken again, with him still in her, and they'd started again.

She'd never known or felt anything like it. But she did know this was how it was meant to be: this was how two became one. Her Mam might have laughed at her for believing in fairy-tales, but now she knew they weren't a fantasy, after all.

But no way would she be telling anyone, anything about this. Not even her best friend. No-one would understand, and the thought of anyone giggling about it....

The way her skin felt, it was like she'd shed the old one. She pressed her fingers against herself, intimately, her lower belly and thighs flooding warm and buttery, remembering his fingers, feather-light and knowing, gradually lifting her to the edge of the world, keeping her hovering there till she thought she'd split in two, then over she went, falling yet somehow rising, pulsating pleasure-waves coursing and tingling like electricity down her legs and up her body, so unbearably exquisite she'd thought she was going to die. Even just thinking about it now brought back an echoing tingle.

And that was when she'd said it. She hadn't planned it, but she couldn't help it. The words had burst out of her just as she was losing herself in that pleasure, when her body was feeling like it was melting into his. And it was true. She had fallen in love with him.

Even if he hadn't said it back, it didn't matter. Men were slower to say these things, but he had to love her or he wouldn't have been like that, so gentle and loving and attentive to every part of her, and not losing control.

If only he'd still been here when she woke up.

Kathy got up, walked naked to the window and parted the curtains. The street-lights were orange-hazed in misty greyness. She wondered if he'd left because they had an early start, or if the day's shooting was some distance away, and wished he'd let her know. Then she thought about going to work. The dreamlike feelings began to dissipate. Despondently, she looked around the room.

His boots were still by the door. Suddenly she realised that the trainers which had been there when they came in were gone.

With a sense of relief, she flopped back onto the bed, remembering him saying something about liking to go running in the mornings. Although after a night like that, she was surprised he had the energy, and a little sad that he did not want to stay and wake up with her. She guessed he must have been gone for about twenty minutes. If she wanted to look halfway decent when he came back, she should wash her hair, at the very least. She jumped off the bed, just as her tummy gave a low, drawn-out rumble.

The idea of breakfast made her think of her Mam, who'd be up shortly to go to work and would find Kathy's bed unslept in. Even though they had a sort of unspoken agreement, her Mam'd be worried. Kathy knew she wouldn't have to say anything if she didn't want to, but this was a small town and even if she sneaked

out the back way, someone was bound to recognise her. Word
would fly round in no time. Maybe it already had. But what did she
care? The thought of giving people something to really wag their
tongues about amused her.

Confronted by her image in the bathroom mirror, Kathy was
shocked. Her hair was a horrible spiky thatch; her face, pale and
blotchy. It was just as well he hadn't stuck around to see this.
Hurriedly, she turned on the shower.

THREE

A pale sandstone outcropping, high as two men, dominates the glade. Rain-furrowed, laced with pale lichen and faint shadows which stretch across its scarred surface, it holds the failing light.

A cloaked figure slowly emerges from the deep shadow cast by the stone, and steps into a pool of soft sunlight. Her hair is tied in a long, thick braid, which glints copper-warm in the mote-filled sunbeam. Her face is illuminated; pale and taut but beautiful.

Thrusting branches aside, another figure breaks free from the shelter of the scrubby, bare trees that crowd up against the rock-wall.

Its tone mellowed by distance, a hunting-horn sounds.

The figure pauses, cocking his dark head as if taking measure of the call. Or maybe of the still woman, who seems unmoved to see the man and remains unmoving as he cautiously approaches her.

The little hollow is sheltered, but a gust of wind tugs at her cloak, revealing a cold glint of silver at her side. She has a dagger in her hand. She is not looking at the man, but beyond him, into the dark of the woodland.

He turns, but there is nothing there. At least, nothing he can see. "Guinevere." He approaches her, his breath misting the cold air. The queen's face softens. "Lancelot. My lord."

A swift movement surreptitiously returns the dagger to its

hiding-place among the folds of her clothing, and she steps forward
and into her lover's arms. Her cold fingers caress his cheek; her
soft, warm mouth presses against his as if she wishes to breathe
him into her.

"I was frightened," she says as she draws back, her face sad.
"You were gone. They all were gone. I was alone. I thought we
were separated for ever."

"I had thought myself free." The knight draws the queen, deepest
love of his richly-destined life, close to him. "But I was never free.
I only wished to end the pain. Never will I let you go again."

"It is too late. They are drawing me home; I hear them, calling...."

Lancelot shakes his head: a slight movement, one of denial.
Cupping her chin, he turns her face up to his and looks into her dark
eyes, but in them sees more than his own reflection. In one swift
movement, he leaps aside, thrusting the woman behind him and
drawing his sword.

Leaning heavily on his staff, a bent figure is standing at the edge
of the trees, watching the tense couple. His robe is threadbare and
grubby with spattered mud, his sparse white hair damp and
straggly. The skin of his face is grey, and sags.

Shivering with cold, or perhaps pain, Merlin treads unsteadily
the serpentine roots of an ancient oak, his left hand reaching out
to support himself, gnarled and knotted as the bark it touches.
As if finding strength there, he stops beneath the great spread of
branches.

"Ghost-born." Lancelot's voice is little more than a whisper. He
takes a step toward the old mage. "Perhaps your magic is less
powerful now. With Arthur lost-"

"Never lost. But sleeping." Merlin shudders as if recalling some
great and terrible deed.

Guinevere lays her hand on Lancelot's arm.

"Stay," she cries. "It is all undone. It is over."

There is a noise like thunder. Exhausted though the three
clearly are, they draw swiftly back, the woman disappearing into a
long fissure in the rock-wall, the magician seeming to meld with

the trunk of the great oak. Only Lancelot is left to face the three horsemen that crash into the clearing.

The sight of the knight, sword at the ready, causes one of the animals to rear and plunge. As its rider struggles to control it, the others leap from their mounts and, howling like dogs, rush at Lancelot, swords in hand.

But one of them stumbles, his foot caught by a tree-root. He falls heavily, leg-bone breaking with a sickening snap as Lancelot steps towards the other, swinging his great, polished sword. His first blow misses, but he darts around the man's wildly thrusting sword and with a great cry lands a telling strike on his opponent's shoulder, cutting through metal and leather, flesh and bone with a hideous, bloody crunch.

Intense and silent, the third intruder rides at Lancelot, the whoosh of his weapon cutting the air beside the knight's head.

"I've lived all my life for this moment!" he screams, flinging himself off his horse.

Lancelot falls back under the force of the fierce onslaught, parrying a clanging hail of thrusts and blows, and stumbles, his guard falling. With a blood-curdling howl, his opponent seizes his advantage and raises his sword. For a long and terrible moment there is silence and stillness: a tableau of imminent death.

Then, with a look of astonishment on his face, one hand grasping futilely at his back, the attacker lets fall his sword and sinks heavily to his knees, his breath rasping.

From between his shoulders protrudes a slim, silver-hilted dagger.

It was the third take that played out as he had imagined. Joe left Jess with the credit and the rest of the crew, and went to look for Melanie, feeling an inexplicable need to talk to her. It took a while, but he finally found her with the owner of the horses. Their heads were close together.

He wasn't surprised. He'd visited her family's big spread in the hills of northern California and seen how the beasts were her first love. Her husband played second fiddle. Waiting for them to finish before he intruded, he stayed at a distance. But before they were done, the horses were being brought back to the trailers to be loaded.

Joe watched carefully. He had never seen a breed like it: wide rumps and powerful shoulders, thick of mane, tails streaming in waves; three of them brazil-nut-brown, gleaming like polished boots. Stocky but spirited animals that easily bore the weight of a man in armour, tossing their heads and snorting plumes of hot breath, stamping feathered hooves in protest against the imminent return to confinement. One he especially liked, a sorrel, heavy-headed, which bounced sideways as it was made to approach the ramp.

Melanie had clearly taken to the white mare, the queen's mount. Hooking the reins through her arm, she took hold of a foreleg and, bracing it firmly on her thigh, began to clean it as the mare ruffled her breath loudly through her nostrils. When she'd done all four, she coaxed her into a trailer. Admiring the light step as the mare pranced inside like a ballet dancer, her finely-sculpted head tucked close into a muscled chest, Joe knew the breed for Arabian.

Remembering his own time with the beasts, Joe knew them for the only beauty in all the years as a ranch-hand. It was not the mastery over them he loved, but the horses themselves, and the power and speed they lent to his own feeble strength. Part of the pattern of life, they had reminded him of his place in it.

They'd woken in him something he'd never known before. Loving to ride bareback, feeling the pull and glide of muscle between his legs, guiding with weight and leg, the horse responding to the will of the small, weak creature on its back. They had brought him solace. He never had to prove himself to them, no more than they to him. They had no need to label, to judge, to condemn. But the liquor had pulled a veil over much of it, as they had over such things before, until he'd barely been able to trust himself, even with the horses.

So much of it now a blur.

Until Lindy. She'd saved him from himself, in a way. He still couldn't account for her interest in him. More than an interest; power enough to get him on the wagon yet again and to marry her. The boss's daughter. That had turned the tables; the hands all had to follow his orders then. And every one of them a whiteman.

Joe shook his head, thinking how things that had once mattered more than anything in the world didn't even touch him any more. There was always something else round the corner. Like this English girl. Only he'd not had this trouble before: not wanting a woman yet being haunted by one. Wanting to be alone, yet not ready to let her go. She'd surprised him, and he had to admit it had been kind of a good thing to come back after a long day and find her still there, waiting for him, wearing one of his shirts, nothing on underneath but his raven, lying between her breasts.

Feeling the flooding warmth of response in his groin, Joe let himself rerun the memory: the soft brightness of her hair against the black of his shirt; the way she'd left the top buttons open, just enough so that the beginning curve of her breasts was visible. His shirt had covered almost half the length of her thighs: a taste, without giving it all away. She'd said nothing but pulled him inside the room and to the bed. He'd allowed her to undress him, her mouth kissing his body as she laid it bare. Watching her from that strange place behind himself, he'd known it for an alcohol-fuelled loss of inhibition; she'd been more cute than sexy, enthusiastically doing everything she knew how until she'd passed out, quite suddenly, and after a few deathly-still moments, started snoring lightly. It had made him smile at the time, and did again now.

He remembered waking early, with her coiled over him. She had a kind of dry warmth that seemed to stretch around him. Then he'd shown her a few things of his own....

It was when he'd come back from his morning run, with his head clear and the intention of keeping his life that way, that she'd announced she couldn't care less about her job. That had made him feel uneasy. But it wasn't his place to tell her what to do.

The horse-trailers were leaving. Unable to work out what he'd wanted to say to Melanie, Joe glanced at the sky and reckoned he had enough space for a smoke before going back.

Heading down towards the river, rolling a neat joint on the way, he thought about how the girl hadn't much cared for him smoking. Even though she hadn't said anything, he could tell. Well, too bad; at least he didn't drink anymore. She wouldn't have liked him then at all; he was a lot mellower with this little helper.

Lighting up in the shelter and privacy of some bushes by the sullen, slow-moving water, Joe took a deep drag and tried to empty his mind.

It had been a strange day. His body was sated, but he felt more than ever aware of himself as observer, only now not only of everything and everybody else, but himself as well. It was as if he was outside of himself. Unsure if it was a distraction, he could feel it beginning to worry him. Was it to do with the sickness in his head? Some kind of next stage? He considered how this was the first time in a long while that a line of work had really touched him, inside, and resolved not to let anything knock him off-track. Having that much straight in his head, he began to feel calmer.

It was good dope, he realised, taking another deep drag. Iain, second camera-man, was taking care of him.

Joe liked it when a man kept his word.

Hearing the key in the front door, Kathy's heart sank. She'd thought late afternoon would be the best bet, with George gone to his evening shift and her Mam not yet home from work. Praying it wouldn't be either of her stepbrothers, just her Mam home early, she hurriedly stuffed the last few things into the hold-all.

Then she heard George's voice. Her throat tightened as she heard his heavy footsteps stomping up the stairs. The door to her room banged open, without so much as a knock.

"So, yer ladyship, what the hell d'ye think this is? Out all hours of the night...."

A fruity-sour smell wafted in with him, turning her stomach. He was not a bad-looking man, but when he drank, his craggy face reddened and often twisted in an ugly way.

From downstairs, she heard her Mam's voice: "George, leave her be."

Kathy knew the best way to handle him was give as good as she got. "Don't start on me. You're always saying the house is too crowded."

"This isn't a fuckin' doss-hoose." Her stepfather advanced a clumsy step. "Ye think ye can just please yersel'..."

"What's your problem?" she shrieked. "You pick on me when I'm here, and now you rant 'cause I'm not! Make up your mind and get off my back. I'm nearly fucking twenty-three! I'm not a little kid!"

"That's obvious to the whole bloody toon! What the fuck d'ye think you're doin? And wi' a Chink, at the Percy," he simpered, then chortled drunkenly. "Does it gan in sideways, like they say?"

"You're an ignorant, bigoted letch." Kathy felt like she might choke with anger. She hated everything about him: the way his trousers cut under his paunch, the seventies' haircut.

"Takes one to knaa one," he sneered. "Ye givin' him a run for his money?" Then he noticed the hold-all. He pointed at it with a limp finger. "What's that aboot?"

"I'm not going to stay here and listen to your filth any more."

"If ye walk oot of here ... don't think ye can come back. Put us all t'shame-"

"As if I'd want to come back. Anyway, Mam-"

"Aye, an' how'll she hold her head up, when ye're gannin' with an old slitty-eyed Chink?"

"He's not Chinese, he's an American Indian."

"Same difference. An' ye might as well know, the bank called. Didn't think I'd lie for ye, did ye?"

"I don't care, I hate that job! And as for holding up anybody's head, I'm not doing anything compared to what your two've got up to. And you're always willing to lie through your teeth for them!

Those people from Newcastle...."

Frowning, George took another step towards her. "Don't ye say nowt about my lads. That wor just a bit of fun-"

"They're psycho. Take after you. At least I pay my way, unlike-"

"Shut yer gob or-"

"Or what? You wouldn't dare lay a finger on me! But maybe that's what...." Kathy stopped herself. She'd never dared go that far before, and hoped her mother hadn't heard. Turning her back, she zipped up her bag firmly and loudly, as a kind of statement. She could hear him, breathing heavily behind her, filling the small room with the stinking fumes of stale beer. She couldn't wait to get out; couldn't think why she hadn't done this a long time ago.

"The old slanty-eyes makin' it worth your while then, lassie?"

"Fancy yourself as a pimp, now?" Hating him more than ever, Kathy pushed past her stepfather.

Her mother was standing at the bottom of the stairs, one hand on the banister, shopping bags round at her feet like a little barricade. Kathy saw she'd had her hair done, but her face looked doughy and grey. She couldn't remember when her mother didn't look tired. Or maybe it was the booze. For the umpteenth time, she promised herself she'd never go that way.

"Don't mind him," her mother said. "You've always had a mind of your own, but you'll always have a home here, no matter what. I don't know what you think you're doing, but just take care, pet. You know what I mean."

Kathy had to smile. She loved her Mam to bits, but her life was a pathetic one. "That's what you always say, Mam."

"I'm just saying, don't throw your life away. Men just use women."

"He's not like that, he's wonderful," said Kathy dreamily. "I'm in love, Mam. Really." She hesitated, dropped her voice to a whisper. "Maybe you could meet him. But only when old fart-face isn't around."

"Love.... You're still so young. And so pretty," said her mother, shaking her head. "More important, what's in the bank. And what about when they leave? American, aren't they?" A sudden thought seemed to strike her, and her eyes widened. "You're not thinking about going there, are you?"

It hadn't been much more than a vague notion in the back of Kathy's mind until that moment, and her first instinct was that she'd never leave her Mam. Then she heard the toilet flush.

"I'm going before the old fart comes down. I'll ring you." Landing a swift kiss on her mother's cheek, Kathy smelled the fresh hairspray. A sudden wave of feeling washed through her. Clutching her bag, she hurried outside.

Guilt trailed after her. How could she leave her Mam on her own with three lazy, drunken louts? But what else could she do? Her mother had made her choice, it was her life. Now she was making her own choice, her own life.

George's voice broadcasted out to the whole street: "You better tell him to watch out. We'll be down there, me 'n' Jimmy 'n' Scotty, and we'll show that slanty-eyed baby-snatcher...."

Kathy made the mistake of looking back. Her stepfather was standing on the stoop, and she would have made a rude gesture except that her Mam was behind him, looking over his shoulder. It was an image that summed up everything about her life that she hated: the stocky, red-haired man in the dark jacket, t-shirt and ill-fitting jeans, filling the doorway; the pale and tired, worried face of her mother peering over his shoulder; the untidy, overgrown, postage-stamp of a front garden; the dingy, cream-and-grey stippled front of the tired old council-house.

Hating her stepfather with a fierceness that made her clench her fists, she turned away and vowed she'd never go back, no matter what. He wouldn't follow through with his threat; he was too selfish, and a coward. His sons were the ones to watch out for, although Scotty had his moments. But only when his brother or father weren't around.

Feeling a growing sense of lightness as she put increasing distance between her and them, and telling herself she couldn't stay home acting as a buffer for her Mam for the rest of her life, she hurried down the hill into town, intending to go back to the hotel and wait for Joe. It was only when she got to the main street that it dawned on her that she'd have to ask at the desk for a key to his room.

Kathy realised she hadn't thought this through at all. Yesterday, while he hadn't said she could wait for him, neither had he said she couldn't. That was one advantage of the way he didn't say much. Waiting for him in the hotel room, reading snippets of long-ago times and watching day-time TV, even plucking up the courage to order from room-service, had been fun, like a little holiday, all the more exciting because of the anticipation of his return. And by the time he'd come back, she'd had her sexy welcome all worked out.

It was just a shame that she'd drunk a bit too much and couldn't remember it clearly. But Joe hadn't sent her away; he'd liked it, or so it seemed, as much as she could remember, and he'd been ready to do it all again in the early morning, when she was quite sober again. And when she'd mentioned she'd like to keep him company while he went jogging in the morning, and would have to go home and get some things, he'd only mumbled something and left. He kept his face so still, it was impossible to know what he was thinking.

Bag in hand, bridges burned behind her and with no idea where they were shooting for the day, Kathy stood indecisively on the edge of the pavement, wondering what on earth she thought she was doing. It had all happened so fast.

She knew she'd lost her job at the bank; they didn't even overlook being late. They'd never take her back now. And now she couldn't go back home. Nor could she have acted any differently. She knew she had to be with him. Even though she didn't know how much longer he'd be working here, or what would happen next, she had to be with him. Shivering with cold, or perhaps from fear or her own daring, she decided she could go to the library to wait out the rest of the day.

Yet, once she was sitting in the warmth with a newspaper on her lap, Kathy found she couldn't concentrate on a word. One hand inside her blouse, she held onto the black bird pendant like a life-line and closed her eyes, losing herself in the images that came into her head: his arm, strong and dark against her white, slim one; the velvety hollow between his neck and the bulge of his shoulder; the expanse of his chest, unmarred by a single hair, like warm marble under her fingers; his nipples, small, hard, dark-brown berries; the thick, black bushiness at the dangly-root of him, which he tucked so nonchalantly into his boxers.

She remembered him walking away from the bed: lean and wiry, buttocks tight and rounded, the palest part of his body; narrow hips; shoulders not wide but strong; the long, narrow valley of his spine; the black flow of hair between his shoulder-blades; the deep scarring on his right calf, about which he still had to tell her. There was so much to find out about him.

She found that if she concentrated very hard on the back passages of her nose and breathed in very, very gently, she could even create a sort of smell-memory: the musky, fresh-cut-grass sweetness of him. It made her go weak with longing.

She'd never known a man could smell so good, body and breath. There was no part of him she didn't love; she'd told him, had shown him, with her mouth and her tongue. The vague memory of some of the things she'd done almost embarrassed her now, but with him, she'd felt beyond herself. Without him, she felt unnatural, incomplete, the emptiness in her chest making it hard to breathe.

She didn't dare let her mind go near the dark edge of the world: what would happen when the filming was completed.

Joe felt the scowl on his face as he headed back to his vehicle. The split inside himself was not a good thing: one part of him going through the motions all day with precision and efficiency, while another part sat somewhere behind this self, impressed with the functions of the robot while it slipped off to circle round moments of the last couple of nights.

Sitting at the wheel, he broke his own rule about smoking in a vehicle and rolled a joint. Taking a deep toke, he tipped back his head and closed his eyes.

An image came to him, from early that morning: the girl, lying in the bath, head dunked underwater, fine, long blonde hair floating round it like a mermaid's; breasts buoyant and pale as her belly; water-darkened bush at the top of her strong thighs....

Shaking his head as if to dislodge the memory, Joe got back out of the vehicle and took several deep breaths. With the next toke, he made his mind spin off and let his gaze follow the huddle of trees retreating up the far side of the hill. At the crest, he registered the gentle movement of the trees, bowing before a vanguard of wind that preceded rain. A distinct grey smudge was sweeping across the hills. He inhaled deeply the kiss of moisture before the wind reached him, whining like a ghost and tugging at his hat. A ragged curtain of cold drizzle followed, a female rain, beading his coat.

He doubted if he could ever adjust himself to the blurred edges, the dim light. He had been getting up before dawn and even though he thought he could feel a song birthing in him, there was never a sun to greet. Despite himself, he again found he was thinking about the girl: how she'd opened to him, clean and bright as a wildflower after rain. A shudder ran through his body.

She did something to him he couldn't understand. It wasn't the sex, although, in pleasuring her, he seemed to lose some part of himself, for a while at least. It was the way she was riding in his mind. Even now, he was wondering where she was. Would she wait for him in his room all day again? He didn't know whether he liked the idea or not, then remembered she'd said something about having to go home.

The joint had gone out. That was a first. To be sure, Joe carefully stubbed it against a dead branch, put it in his pocket, got into his vehicle and decisively started the engine.

Even as he drove, the girl kind of haunted him: lurking in the shadowy recesses of his head and, although his mind was busy with the driving and reflections on the day's work, she was leaking in through the spaces. He'd never known anything like it; it was like she was putting a spell on him, seducing and corrupting the general ordering of his life, which he'd only just begun to bring back into balance.

Like one of the Old Testament heroines he'd read about, he thought, seducing and bewitching the foreign despot who held her people in slavery. Until the opportunity came for the dagger across the throat, the nail in the head.

Joe smiled to himself, wondering at the way his mind sometimes ran.

If he saw her again, all he had to do was let slip a few truths about himself and his life; she'd be turned off, pretty quick. She'd said some fanciful things, like "meant to be", but he would show her how the stuff she'd conjured up in her head was not about him at all. It was his own fault.

Or Jay's. She'd been a good training-camp.

This English girl was young, and in a hokey little place like this, most likely never had a sexual experience anything near what he'd given her. And his escape clause was in hand. So what was he getting worked up about? Because she had the guts to throw over a job? Act on the moment? He had to admire that; it was the sort of thing he'd used to do.

In any case, she was probably gone. If she wasn't, he'd take care to do it gently. He knew better than to leave a trail of negativity behind him.

Reaching the hotel, Joe found himself driving past it, his talisman now at the front of his mind. He'd never guessed she'd put it on; she'd clearly thought it had been a gift. But it was one of only two things that held any sort of value to him, and he regretted the impulse. What had made him do it? He remembered not wanting to disturb her, lying deeply asleep in a tangle of sheets, knowing she'd probably never had a night like that before and maybe never would again, and the upwelling of tenderness which had made him cover her up. But leaving his bolo in case she woke up while he was gone had been taking it too far; she'd been wearing it when he got back from the run, and it wasn't his way to ask for things back. Not even when he'd had the opportunity at the end of that day, when she'd still been there.

It irritated him that it should still be on his mind: it meant he hadn't been able to let it go. He'd used to mock whiteman and his belongings; whiteman, belonging to nothing, who was always creating things, making things to belong to him. Thinking he owned them, when in truth, they owned him.

Although it still wasn't clear: was it really about the trinket? Or was it about the girl? Or his own needs, which he'd thought he'd tamed?

Hearing those words had affected him, even though he knew that saying such things in the heat of the moment meant nothing, especially when it was a young girl with no experience. All the same, it had been both flattering and kind of disturbing. Love. He'd managed to block it out at the time, or he might not have been able to continue.

Anyway, he thought dismissively, he knew the type: thinking she was feeling love, she'd be like a leech if it went any further, and expecting him to start saying things he didn't feel.

Finding himself beyond the town and in the countryside again, Joe pulled up and turned off the engine. The vehicle already smelled of dope; one more won't hurt, he decided. This time he rolled a very slim joint.

Feeling the chemical reach his brain, he became aware of the soft relaxation of his mind, expanding, and sat back and waited for the day to lose the rest of its light. It happened slowly in this wintry, northern land; the sky always overcast, the sun perpetually struggling to make its presence known.

On reflection, he knew it had been a good day. Owen had been in unusually high spirits, his wit sharp and subtle. And the shooting had gone well, they'd cleared the day's schedule. Even if his mind had wandered, it hadn't affected his work; the energy he'd felt in the morning run had been strong all day, staying with him. Although if he were true to himself, toking up and getting into shape was living a lie. He knew that if he just steeled himself for a while to get into the way of it, he could stop with the weed.

Stubbing out the joint, he decided the raven was a small price to pay. They'd both had a good time; she had a keepsake. She didn't know what it meant. Best to put her feelings and the thing out of his mind altogether and just let time spin out.

Starting up the engine again, Joe pulled the jeep round and drove back through the dark with the windows open, until the pungent smell dissipated and his mind emptied. Nevertheless, when he finally got back to the hotel, a nebulous feeling dogged his steps. He shook it off, telling himself it was wisest to get an early night. Yet he found himself checking the bar before he went up to his room.

Kathy's head was full of sounds, like echoes in a valley whispering and fading on the wind. Eyes closed, she remained still, matching her breathing to the rhythmic rise and fall of Joe's chest, acutely aware of every nuance: his cool breath on the back of her neck, the warmth radiating from his stomach against her lower back, his arm heavy over her waist, hand curled under her breast, the greater weight of his body, anchoring her to him.

Although she felt she couldn't be happier, something kept her from falling asleep. One of the bedside lights was on – he liked it that way – but that wasn't what was keeping her so wide awake.

It had been worth the long wait, even in the dark, the library long closed, until her freezing hands and feet had forced her into the hotel, feeling horribly conspicuous and trying to keep the bag hidden behind a chair when the sudden, loud clamour of American accents had disrupted the quiet of the lobby, making her heart leap and her stomach start to flutter. But Joe hadn't been with them, and they'd walked past her as if she didn't exist. The time dragged, and she'd moved into the bar when it opened and nursed an orange juice for an age. Eventually, some of the Americans left again.

That was the moment Joe had appeared, in his long, black coat, his black hat at a slight angle. She'd never forget the way he'd looked straight at her for a long moment, his eyes black and unfathomable. He'd said nothing, but picked up her bag and carried it upstairs, as if he'd been expecting her.

Languidly, Kathy stretched her legs. She could hardly tell where her body ended and his began.

To be kissed like that: lips telling each other the story of who they were. And what had he said somewhere in all of that, which had almost made her melt?

"The sacred wind of your life I breathe."

She repeated the words softly to herself. It was the most beautiful, poetic, intimate thing she could imagine. Not for the first time, she wished she'd been a virgin; that she'd waited for him so he could be her first. And only. Instead, her virginity had been tossed away like small change behind the couch at a party; so drunk she'd barely noticed Billy had gone all the way, and because there'd been no blood, he hadn't believed it when she insisted he was her first and had dumped her. She remembered crying herself practically deaf, but now it seemed like it had happened to someone else, light-years ago.

But Joe ... she'd never known a man could be so sensitive; that such strong hands could be so gentle. He made love like he played the flute: breathing into it, touching it so lightly, enticing from it soft sounds. Some of their love-making she couldn't remember at all; she'd never known she could be made to feel like that: sort of exposed and vulnerable, yet quite safe. She loved the weight of him on her, the way he filled her. They were a perfect fit. And he could go on for ages, which she thought was fantastic; she'd never had a real lover, one who could control himself and make sure she was satisfied first.

The only trouble was, Kathy realised, she hadn't been able to tell when, or even if, he'd come. Understandable the first couple of times; she barely knew him. And then she'd got herself stupidly drunk, and couldn't remember much about what had happened that night at all.

It was sort of strange. She'd never had to think about it before, it had always been obvious: a frenzied, thumping race to the end, some death-like groaning and moaning and a wilting-away. Joe hadn't done any of that, and whenever they drew apart, he was almost always hard, and stayed that way for a long while. If they'd have used something, she'd have known, but she hadn't wanted to spoil the spontaneity, the closeness. And the thought of the risk – if it could be called a risk, so close to her period – both thrilled and scared her. Imagining the child they'd have together, she fantasised about blonde with dark eyes, raven-haired with blue....

Then it hit her: maybe he was holding back to make sure that that wouldn't happen.

Although it made sense that he was simply taking responsibility, Kathy felt saddened. She wanted to risk all. Squeezing the warm hand that cupped her breast, she encountered the hard lump of his signet ring.

It wasn't a wedding ring; he'd told her that much. She'd been so relieved. If he was married, she wouldn't have known what to do, how to be.

Snaking her hand behind her back and down between their bodies to touch him, she felt a familiar twinge in her lower belly. Her Mam had always said there was nothing like "a good steamy session to get things going", but she couldn't help feeling a little disappointed: one possible avenue had been removed.

Fondling him absentmindedly, she felt how, even asleep, he was beginning to respond. Resolving that getting her period wouldn't change anything, that she could still show him how she loved him in all kinds of other ways, Kathy noted the slight change in his breathing as he tightened his grip on her breast, and knew he was awake now, too.

"There's some things you oughta know 'bout me, English." Joe's voice was husky.

Thrilled that he must at last be starting to open up, Kathy wriggled round to face him without letting go of him. With the fingers of her other hand, she combed back his hair, loving the sleek silkiness of it. But he seemed distracted; was softening under her fingers.

"I want to know everything about you," she said, fighting back a feeling of foreboding.

"You might regret sayin' that, wench." Joe sensed from her sudden tension that he'd come across too heavy. Or maybe it was because of naming her in that way: words that emphasised the chasm that lay between them.

"I doubt it," she said. "Anyway, you know all about me, while I know hardly anything about you. I know more about the movie, than I do about you. Sometimes it's like you use it as a shield."

Joe lay back, crossing his hands under his head, and looked up towards the ceiling. Without him realising it, one of his feet began to twitch rhythmically.

"And in any case, the past's just that: history," the girl rattled on. "But I want to know. Like, tell me about where you're originally from."

Glad of the dim light, Joe wished she could just wait it out until he was ready to speak. Did she think he needed her promptings? "Empty desert."

"Come on, you can do better than that. I'm really interested."

Closing his eyes, Joe let the images rise in his mind's eye until he felt them in the warm flesh of his body, in the dark blood coursing through his veins, and in the long, dry purity of his bones. Then the words came, telling of an arid, austere, broken, sandstone and shale country, where the wind howled and moaned among sandblasted towering cliffs, gusts and eddies snatching up the red dust and moulding it into blood-coloured dust-devils that chased through the flat alluvial valleys, dying away before they reached the deep, mysterious gorges, basins and crevasses. He painted a picture of the brightly-coloured mesa: dark-red igneous rock, glaring-white limestone, dull-yellow granite; the sunsets, a sear of vermilion-crimson, an angry red flare, a flush of delicate rose; copper-coloured twilights. He recalled the rolling upland plains, high, pine-clad mountains, scanty vegetation, rough grass and stretches of sage brush, groves of stunted pinyon and juniper trees. Thunderheads building high over the mesa, yet how rain might not come for months. How the air was thin at such a high altitude: clean, and dry.

"Not many people can live in a place like that," he reflected. "Reminds a man how small and weak a thing he is in the order of things.... An' where I'm from, they're superstitious. Still believe in things like werewolves." He laughed, but it was a short, bitter laugh.

"Not all that long ago," the girl said softly, "people here used believe the countryside was haunted by witches, evil spirits."

Joe stayed quiet for a while, unsure whether that was all she wanted to say; wishing he hadn't lost himself in the telling and given quite so much.

"My life's a small thing," he said eventually, realising he didn't really want to say anything more. But this was a thing he had started. "For many years ... liquor had a tight hold on me, spoiled my thinkin'."

He waited again for a few moments, but she had nothing to say about that. "Only got clear 'cause of a good woman. An' the smoke, that helps."

Again he sensed her tension. She had questions, probably to do with what he'd said about Lindy. Although they were always curious, women didn't really like hearing about the other ones. He decided to get it over with.

"Didn't have much truck with schoolin', an' the liquor was always there...." He stopped, considered, then continued: "Not much of that time I can recall, but one thing for sure, it wasn't pretty. Learned in the military the way you get respect is by bein' tougher than the next guy. An' that ... well, the price of a life ain't cheap.... Worked awhile breakin' horses, then things changed, for a time. But even a woman like that, an' a kid, that wasn't enough to keep me straight, 'though I thought at first...." Joe stopped. His voice had become gruff, and his way of speaking was beginning to revert to something he thought he'd left behind.

"What made you start, you know, drinking?" The girl's voice was neutral.

Trying to deal with the thoughts and images beating heavy round his head like buzzards, Joe was silent. He heard the girl take a deep breath.

"My dad was an alcoholic," she continued, very quietly. "My real dad, I mean. He's Irish. A musician. Plays in a band. The fiddle, and some acoustic guitar. Folk music, mostly, the old music.... Or at least he used to. I don't know what he does now; even if he's alive. I've only got some vague memories of him singing and stuff. He and Mam weren't married, and when I appeared on the scene, well, he couldn't handle the responsibility. I was about three when he ran off, and as far as I know, he never got back in touch. I think ... well, it was hard for Mam, working and all. We had to go and live with my Nan and Granddad. They needed help to manage by then. Although it was okay having Nan to come home to, after school. Then George came along.... He was okay in the beginning. But I think he only really took up with Mam 'cause he needed someone to take care of him and his boys, you know? The way he treats her ... I mean, it's not like he beats her up, but she has to do everything like he wants. And she has to work and he never lifts a finger round the house. None of them do...."

Joe could tell she'd started out trying to help him out, but she was rattling again. Some things were better kept private, he thought.

"Liquor on my side, too," he nonetheless offered in return. "Mostly raised by my mother's mother. Kind of a tradition, I guess. Till she got too old. Or I got too much of a handful."

He felt her hand lightly touch his chest.

"I know how hard it can be," she said softly. "So, how did you stop the drinking?"

He closed his eyes. Painfully it came out: "A woman. It was always a woman."

Why he was telling her any of this?

Even though she knew it was irrational, Kathy didn't like how she was feeling about all these women before her. "Um, why I asked about it ... well, in my experience, alcohol's used by people who're deeply unhappy and angry about their life, you know?"

"An' how come you're so wise, li'l English?"

Joe's tone was harsh, but she was used to how emotional the issue was. "I told you. I had to live with it, too. George. And he calls my real Dad 'the pickled pikey', whenever he can. Talk about pot calling the kettle black. Mind you, I called him 'Whisky Mac'. 'Cause he's got ginger hair and he's half-Scots, you see...."

That usually made people laugh, but this time it seemed to go down like a lead balloon.

"Look, none of that makes any difference," she continued. "I take people as they come. And I don't care what other people say, either.... I mean, you're a long way from that time, you know? And look how you're doing now. I mean, with the movie and all...."

Kathy decided she'd had enough for now, even though she felt little the wiser and there were enormous holes in his life-story. The best bit had been in the beginning, when he'd told her about the place where he grew up.

Then she found herself wishing she hadn't told him so much about what it was like at home. It had been bad enough telling him about the reaction when she'd gone home for her things, and George's threat. For a few seconds, she'd been aware of something behind Joe's expression, something that made her blood run cold. Not fear, she knew. It had been a darkness, a hard sort of shadow. It had been scarier than if he'd threatened out loud to go over and do George, and the memory of it still made her feel strange.

Nor had he said anything about her idea of staying on for a couple of days till she worked something out. Although she wouldn't have had to say that, if only he'd offered.

But there was no point in going there. As it was, he'd been really generous, pulling fifty quid out of his wallet, just like that, and telling her to get whatever else she needed.

Raising herself on one elbow, Kathy looked down at Joe. His eyes were closed. Even when he was relaxing in bed, his face was hard as a piece of seasoned firewood. Two lines ran from the edge of his nose to the corners of his mouth, as if cut by a knife. Over his temple, like a bolt of lightning, ran a jagged scar. Wondering what had caused it, she felt something soften within her. His face was so extraordinary, she felt she could look at it forever.

Slipping her hand under the sheets, barely touching him, Kathy ran her fingertips down his thigh and then slowly, tantalisingly, back up towards his groin.

"Maybe," she turned on her sexy voice, "I can make you forget there ever was a past. Maybe it all begins now, from this very moment."

Feeling embarrassed, she hesitated. She'd never said anything like that to anyone before. Then she heard him give a long sigh. One of pleasure, it seemed, from the way he was responding to her deft and seductive fingertips, which seemed to be operating of their own volition, knowing exactly what to do.

FOUR

Like harried ghosts, streaks of cloud race across a slate-coloured sky, made pale by the full moon. The wind in the trees roars like distant sea-surge; bare branches clack a dry-bone dance. The sole stillness among the mayhem is a stone tower, lit cold and stark by bright moonlight, raising its forbidding mass above the trees.

At its foot, four heavily-cloaked figures crouch round a small fire. In the dark wildwoods beyond them, shadowy forms shift, an enigmatic and disquieting movement beyond the mad flickering cast by the flames.

The fire gutters and flattens. One of the figures gets up, and pokes at the coals.

The wind gusts and the fire flares, lighting up strong, rough features, bushy eyebrows and moustache, an unshaven jaw. A wavering, elongated scarecrow-shadow is thrown against the rough stone wall behind him.

The wind tugs at the man's cloak, and he wraps it closer, pulling the hood over his head.

In that moment, a shadowy something unpeels itself from the underbrush at the edge of the circle of firelight and with an obscene, piercing shriek, throws itself on him.

Struggling to free himself from the creature clinging to his back like a burr, the man stumbles backwards through the fire, his boots kicking up embers which are snatched by the wind and tossed in the air, a glowing swirl that twinkles briefly like fireflies and disappears.

Pandemonium breaks loose as more dark shapes detach from shrub and tree and fall in a frenzy upon the other men, shrieking like animals in torment, an unearthly, inhuman sound.

The cold light of the moon, and the all-too-human screams as sword and dagger take their toll, reveal the ghostly attackers to be small, wild-haired, fur-clad men and women with blue-painted faces. Fiercely they struggle with the cloaked men, and then suddenly it is over.

Three cloaked figures stand by the scattered remains of the fire, chests heaving, plumes of hot breath streaming from nose and mouth. One clutches a limp and useless arm. At their feet lie half a dozen humped forms, one of them moaning in a terrible way.

"By the blessed Mother! Lancelot!" cries one of the men, falling onto his knees by a still figure that lies near the fire, the edge of his cloak smouldering.

"Yeah! Cut!" Jess punched the air. "Now that's more like it. You guys deserve a medal."

Standing behind Camera One, arms folded over his chest, Joe nodded in appreciation, looking up at the moon.

Its clear fullness, and the powerful, gusting wind.... He saw both as a gift; the people had only had to work with the elements. Glad his suggestion of a subtle adjustment to the lighting had been taken up, he could see that it had added to the eerie quality of the scene, at least from Camera One's viewfinder, behind which he'd been standing throughout the take. With all three cameras rolling, he knew there'd be choice material to work with.

Noting the solicitous attention being paid to Brandon, who was taking his time getting up, Joe had to smile. The unplanned sacrifice of Lancelot's cloak had been a neat touch.

Dwelling on the way women of the ancient northern tribes-people had fought side-by-side with their men, he let his mind relive the dark beauty of the scene, to be taken aback when the bodies began to rise again from death and pick up their weapons. A shiver ran up his spine.

Turning away from the disintegrating death-scene, he swept his gaze over the huddle of people gathered behind the arc lights. Blinded to detail, he could sense she was there, despite the cold.

Bringing her along had gone against his instincts, but it would have been impolite to leave the girl behind again, knowing now some of what had shaped her. Learning more than he might have wished ... he'd had to look away from the pain and shame in her face when she'd told him about her family. Even though he had known far worse, he felt for her.

And although he was well practised in not allowing his mind to go that way, a thought surfaced: how did Evie remember him? Did she ever speak of her father? Was her voice filled with pain; her face covered with shame?

A sudden, darker thought struck him: was this why he hadn't been able to move the English girl on? Because of some crazy, twisted connection with his own daughter?

Darkness roared in Joe's head. He wanted to be alone. But that would mean being alone with his mind, increasingly running away on itself. He had to bring his thoughts into line.

Evie, he knew, looked nothing like this English girl. His daughter carried his skin, his eyes, his hair. He remembered his amusement at how his genes had won out, when he first saw her. That had been a good time, although it was hard to remember much of it now.

This Kathy was pale of skin and hair and eyes, and a few seasons older. In fact, her age was somehow crazily mixed: green like spring, grey like winter. Her life seemed to have been one of caring for others: her mother, her grandparents.

He remembered her saying that hiding in a bottle was like a sickness – a truth he knew only too well – yet she had love for her father. Or at least the idea of him. Why had her father not taken care of her?

He recalled how his own ambivalence had been swept away when he'd held his daughter for the first time and realised the fragile nature of early life: the total dependence of such a small and helpless creature. It hadn't been all that long before she was ruling him, and most everyone else. Which was when the tables had been turned and Lindy had begun her slow journey backwards, down into that beginning, helpless state. It had been unbearable to watch; he'd already seen death rising in her, before the useless treatments turned her into a pale and gaunt shadow of the vibrant woman she had been. Unable to stick around to the bitter end, he'd known Evie'd be fine with her maternal grandparents. It was natural, like the old way: the old ones always did a better job with the little ones.

This Kathy had been as an old one, he realised. A child giving support to her elders. The old order, turned on its head. A child's due was love, security and support, given by her elders.

With a grimace, he understood how things seemed to have turned a circle: the now was bringing a haunting echo of the past. What did this mean?

Hearing his name being called, Joe saw he was being beckoned over by Ray. Jess, Melanie and Brandon were with him. He knew what it would be about: even though he had approved it, Jess would pick apart the scene, for no reason other than the sound of his own voice and need to show who was in control.

But even as things unfolded as he'd anticipated, Joe appreciated being freed from the mad birds beating in his brain.

When, without any gain, the little head-to-head was over, Joe headed over to the tree-line for a quick smoke. Once there, realising he'd become too aware of things he'd used to do without thinking, as a kind of offering, he discarded the rest of his stash among the tree-roots, then gazed over the dappled-silver fields and shadowy woods and back up at the hulking ruins of the abbey.

Here, in the lee of the hill, the wind barely touched him, but he could hear it soughing through the higher branches like ghosts moaning to be freed from their wandering.

Owen had told him it was possible the abbey had been built on a much older sacred place. Joe had appreciated the idea of layer upon layer of spiritual focus, the land holding its memory and its truth, changing form as the perception of the people changed. Whiteman was only responding in his own way to a greater truth.

But now, he could only sense loss, emptiness.... He thought how people fought over what they called sacred; how many ended their lives for a simple truth that was in everything, everywhere. It felt to him that their pain and sadness, their separation, was all gathered back together, this night, in this place.

Scurrying clouds chased across the pale face of the moon, eerie shapes torn to rags as they fled. Watching them, Joe waited until his mind was quiet again and the last of the gear was packed away and the vehicles were beginning to drive off.

By then, he'd almost forgotten about the girl, whom he found curled up in the back of his vehicle with a book, reading by flashlight, her long, pale hair hiding her face and falling softly over the familiar patterning of the blanket she'd wrapped herself up in. Woven in an orange, turquoise and white geometric design, it had been a gift when he'd married the first time, and was the only other thing he had felt to keep. Like his raven, it had always travelled with him, keeping many backs warm. Even to England, now. Only it looked like the raven might get to stay behind....

She said nothing when he got in beside her about how long she'd been waiting or how he was always last to get back, but simply looked up and smiled and put a hand on his arm. Glad of her patience and acceptance, he managed not to reflexively recoil from the sudden touch, but the effort cost him. For when she pulled open the blanket and his eyes fell on her naked body, the only stab at modesty some skimpy black lace pieces, he was unable to react at all. Such brazen lack of modesty was something he probably would never get used to.

"Come on in; the water's warm...." Her voice was husky and breathy.

She's trying for Marlene Dietrich, a little voice in his head commented.

Joe had to look away. To him, her face and body looked ghostly, a combination of the moonlight and the small, artificial light of the vehicle. It was life, devalued.

"Hey, what's the matter?" Her question followed him like a dart. "Don't like what you see?"

Her tone was petulant; he was aware she'd covered herself again. Now would come the scene; the roles to be played out. And he'd promised himself: never again. How would he overcome this weakness? Just ride it through for the moment, he thought. Let it disintegrate. Let it go.

"Say something," she demanded. "You always make me fill in the spaces."

What was there to say?

"See? You're doing it again," she cried. "And you know something? You never really look at me, either, not even with this on offer...." She indicated her covered body. "When we're talking, you're always looking over my shoulder, like you're not interested or there's something more important there. Sometimes you even close your eyes when I'm speaking. Is it that bad, looking at me, looking into my eyes?"

Joe thought how he'd used his eyes to great effect on her at least a couple of times. Although he'd had to overcome something in himself to do it. He doubted if he could ever learn to do this thing in what whiteman might say was a natural way.

Weary, reluctant to engage, he nevertheless found some words: "It's in me, not to look at someone directly when they're talkin'. It's just polite."

"But it feels like you're sort of, like, evading me. Or you're not really interested, except for...." She looked down, tracing around the serrated edges of the four-pointed stars that were scattered into the design of the blanket, and, after a while, sniffed.

So she hadn't been waiting so patiently after all, he thought. And she was crying for herself, he knew that, but felt he owed it to her to explain.

"The way I was raised ... it's an invasion of personal space, readin' non-verbal signals." He laughed curtly. "They taught us in school: tradition is the enemy of progress. Give up the old ways, or die. Guess you could say I'm a backwards kinda guy."

The girl was silent. Joe watched a luminescent drop of water making its languorous way down the inside of the misted window. Suddenly, unexpectedly, images were crowding in his mind: a coppery splash of blood on yucca leaves, soaking into the grit; one white trainer, an incongruous presence on the edge of the highway; the long, deep ruts left by the out-of-control pick-up. He could barely even remember her name ... Annie. They had been married only a couple of months. He'd been too drunk to feel much then, and couldn't, after, and would never, now. He was a curse to all the women he took up with.

"It's like learnin' to live with an arrow through your heart."

Shocked at how his mouth had spoken without knowing it was going to, Joe closed his eyes. A tightening began in his head. He barely recognised his own voice: "There's no half-way. Try that, you get tore apart. Never did learn why ... been runnin' ever since. It's not a good way to live.... Uh, there's somethin' wrong in my head." A double-flash pierced the front of his skull, making it feel like it was about to split open.

Resentment curled hot and rough in Joe's throat. He'd thought keeping a lid on it all had become like a second skin. He did not need a woman to remind him of who he was. When he felt the girl's hand touch his shoulder, he roughly shrugged himself away.

Instead of retreating, however, she moved her hand to his neck and pressed gently against it. Her touch was light, her fingers cool. So maybe that was why he did nothing but sit, unmoving, like a rock, when he should have been getting to his pills. It felt good, and for one long, dangerous moment he almost gave way, almost let himself fall.

At that moment, he became aware of a strange noise, like the humming of bees. It was something new, and it was not in his head.

He would have opened his eyes, except he knew it would only make things worse. Then he realised it was the girl; he could feel the vibration through her hand.

What did she think she was doing?

He heard a faint click; behind his closed eyes, was aware of darkness. Despite the pressure in his head and another flicker of light stabbing hot behind his eyes, he was intrigued.

It seemed to be some kind of song she was humming, soft, melodious. Maybe she had some of her father's gift, if unpractised.

He felt her other hand on his forehead, and her fingers and thumb began to slide back and forth above his eyebrows, first lightly, then with more pressure. The hand on the back of his neck matched the movement. The humming seemed to be travelling down her arms, through her hands and into his head, and was unexpectedly soothing. Certainly, it was enough to keep him from telling her to quit. He'd never liked the idea of massage, but this was nothing like he'd imagined.

After a while, he felt her shift her position. Without interrupting the humming or the contact, she arranged herself so she was kneeling astride him. But it wasn't at all sexual. Her fingers, warming and steady, moved to his temples, where she used the heels of her hands to knead the skin, pulling it back, down and round, while she still hummed the strange tuneless, wordless song.

The next few spears of light seemed to be getting duller, although they still made him wince. And as she continued this odd kind of massage over the top and down the back of his head and on to his neck and shoulders, then back to the beginning, again and again, he could feel the immanence in his head beginning to recede, as if she were drawing out the darkness, the tension.

He'd never experienced anything like it; the thought of witches entered his mind. Although he knew he could easily push her away, he felt powerless, his body increasingly languid. Almost, he fell asleep.

Her scent wafted warm in his nostrils, and to his immense surprise, he felt a hot surge in his lower belly, a pressing need that came from seemingly nowhere. Unable to stop himself, he grasped at the girl's waist.

Encountering her bare skin, smooth and cool, Joe felt his excitement escalate. The blanket had fallen off her. He opened his eyes.

In the bright moonlight, she looked like an ice-maiden, sculpted and pale. He pulled her to him, pressing his face against the cool softness of her breasts and breathing in the sweet-woman aroma of her. He could feel himself straining for her, and felt that if he waited any longer, not just his head but his whole body would explode.

The humming stopped, and the girl giggled softly, like a naughty child. He knew she would think she had control. But it didn't matter.

Barely knowing what he was doing, silencing the inner, watching, critical part of him, Joe ran his hands over the silky smoothness of her hips and buttocks. Unable to understand how he had allowed it to come to this, he only knew that never before had he wanted so desperately to enter into the domain of woman. She was trying to kiss him but he barely noticed; he was aware only of one destination, one purpose. He unzipped himself.

The sudden exposure to the cold air only added to his desire. Hooking the ridiculously tiny, black-lace thong to one side with his fingers, he rose into her, feeling the chafe of the material, then, meeting the hot, sleek, wet kiss of her, pulled her down, hard, so he was lost in the sweet tightness.

A groan sounded, loud in the confined space.

It was his own, pressed out of him, as much pain as pleasure. His lower body felt so full, he dared not move, and he grasped her hips so she could not either.

"Lose yourself in me, in the secret, dark cave that is woman. I am the ocean from which you began...."

He'd never heard a woman speak like that before. Dizzily, he felt a surge of response in the throbbing fullness at his groin. It was as if he were rising to meet himself.

"I am the river for you to drown in, lose yourself in, make you forget all that went before...."

Her voice seemed to come from very far away. In his mind's eye, he moved from the darkness of the cave to the brightness of floodwaters seething through a narrow canyon, to pool behind the great wall of a dam.

The waters were too great, too powerful; the dam could not hold.

Something seemed to crack. With a cry that was wrenched from the core of his body, Joe felt a monumental inner collapse and a simultaneous sweet, hot, blossoming-bursting-tingling that convulsed his body and swooped down his legs and into his feet while sweeping him upwards into an excruciatingly bright core of light as his groin twisted, shuddered and pulsed with a pain-pleasure so exquisite and extended, that he lost all thought.

Joe clung to her, rocking and moaning with the intensity of it, his heart banging inside his ribs as the pulsing gradually ebbed, leaving his limbs and body weak and his body tingling.

Chest aching, filled with wonder and at the same time emptied and sad and helpless, he remembered to breathe again. The muscle in the back of his right leg spasmed, and to his horror, tears sprang to his eyes. He couldn't help it. He began to weep, helplessly, silently.

The girl stayed unmoving, holding him inside her, kissing his forehead softly, starting again with that weird humming and stroking the back of his neck and his head. It was like she was going back to the beginning, starting all over again. And he was afraid that he wouldn't be able to survive it. Nor could he let her know of his tears.

He turned his head to one side, swallowed hard and, squeezing his eyes, shut off the flow.

She mustn't know he'd lost control; he could never tell her how he hadn't released into a woman for more years than he could remember. If she knew the power she had over him, a power which had crept up like the shadow of night stealing across the land, she might gorge on him, become fat on his flesh. He couldn't allow it.

Feeling something like revulsion, he almost pushed her away.

Yet the fit of himself inside her, even now; the curve of her body, softly-yielding and warm; the pulsing pleasure echo in his groin ... all conspired to hold him there. His energy was totally drained.

Or was it the girl; had she drained him?

"Who are you?" Joe found himself asking. The spasm in his leg was reborn as a cramp, making it jerk of its own accord, as if trying to buck her off.

She climbed off and cuddled up to him, spreading the blanket across both their lower bodies.

"The one you came here to find."

Her tone was deep, theatrical. But part of him wanted to believe it.

"That's what you said once, remember? Or something like it," she added in a normal voice, pulling the blanket closer round herself.

Glad of the darkness, Joe bent over to rub the tightly-knotted muscle in his leg, using the opportunity to dry away his tears on the blanket.

His own role-playing, he thought as he zipped himself up again, back to haunt him. Something about her had changed. Did she realise what had happened? The significance? Yet how could she? He felt as if his mind were filling with sand.

"It's destiny," she was continuing, "us being together. Whatever went before, whatever you were or did, it doesn't matter, except that it brought you here. And to think how easily we might have missed each other, you know?" Placing a hand on his chest, she laid her head beside it. Her voice dropped to a whisper. "I never even knew they were advertising for extras. And it was someone I don't get on with at all that told me about it.... You know, that first day, I almost didn't stick it out. I was going home when I heard your flute.... I'll never forget that: I couldn't resist. And there was something about you, too, from the very first time I saw you, when we first got there.... It has to be fate."

Joe's heart-beat was slowing. Naturally sceptical of coincidence, he was reminded of Jay. She'd said something like this when they were first together, and he'd wanted to believe her: such a beautiful, intelligent woman. But soon as the ring was on her finger, she'd begun telling him what she liked, what she wanted. Then demanding it, as a right. He'd lost himself to her power for a while. Maybe that was why she'd moved on; she needed challenge. It was how she'd come to be such a high-class lawyer. But he'd been left with some new tools. He'd learned how to manipulate women to comply with his own need.

Yet even though he had realised the sickness of his mind, his heart, and recognised the need for change, he'd still fallen back into the old patterning, the pattern for his own being that he'd seen in his father.

But now, something had changed: this was the first time in over twelve years he'd been able to let himself go inside a woman.

Only it hadn't been about allowing; he hadn't had any choice.

The girl was curled against his body, warm and still. He rested his head against hers. Her damp hair smelled sweet and salty at the same time. He couldn't remember having put it there, but his arm was round her shoulder, the marriage-blanket a familiar presence under his cupped hand.

She'd only been in his life for a few days, but he'd noticed how small things were beginning to affect him: the fact that she'd stopped wearing perfume when he'd said he preferred her natural scent; the small space her few clothes took up in the closet; the tiny, black lace panties, drying on the shower-rail; her small new runners side-by-side with his large, battered ones; her determination to go out and run with him that morning, even in the darkness, the cold and rain. And the uncanny way she'd sometimes say something that had just been a thought in his own mind.

Sometimes, it was good not to be alone.

His mind was becoming sluggish and his body felt soft and weak. An echo of the pain inside Joe's head twinged briefly; then light exploded inside his head. It turned blood-red, and he began to fall through the darkness.

He turns, and is shocked to discover a black hole beside his head. It is just big enough for him to squeeze through, head first. He is in an underground tunnel, narrow, dark and winding, taking him deeper and deeper. Afraid to go on, he knows he cannot go back but has to continue.

Light returns, cool and green. Long rays of sunlight flicker downwards like soft searchlights. He is underwater, sinking slowly, like a dead body. He holds his breath as long as he can, then to his relief finds he can breathe, like he is sucking air out of the water.

White shells lie on the sea-bed below him. Through the green gloom, shadows are moving, swimming towards him. He wonders how he will defend himself, but the massive dark creature passes him by, one great cold eye staring at him.

Progress is very slow, his attempts to swim slow and clumsy, as if he is boneless. Then he sees his hands have turned to flippers, which so frightens him that he pushes for the surface.

Joe opened his eyes to darkness, gasping, his heart thudding, his hands pushing at the weight of the water, which turned out to be the blanket.

"What was that about?" Kathy's voice was filled with laughter. "Did you dream? 'Cause you just gave an almighty twitch!"

Joe wasn't even aware he had fallen asleep. But to his surprise, the headache was gone.

The images and sensations in his dream-state crowded, still strong, into his mind. Water was a new element, one to which he had never been attracted. The eye of the huge water-creature seemed somehow burned into his brain. He knew this to be a dream of some significance, but he couldn't sift through it with the girl poking at him, laughing at him.

Untangling himself from her limbs, he muttered something about needing a real night's sleep, climbed into the front and started up the engine.

He seemed to know the way better than she did, even though she'd grown up here.

In the darkness and mist, it was even more of a challenge to keep up with Joe. Kathy followed him, watchfully negotiating the ruts, greasy with mud and treacherous with stones. They followed the back lane until it led into a field. The grass was long and wet, and the lower legs of her pants soon became saturated. A heavy cotton mix, they became heavier and heavier until the weight began to pull them down over her hips. She had to pull them up at the waist every so often, which slowed her down even more.

At the end of the field, Joe lightly sprang over a gate while she had to use the stile, but she was glad he was in front when he ran on and almost into a small herd of sturdy, long-haired brown cattle, some of them with sweeping horns, who scattered at his confident whoop, tails high as they disappeared into the greyness.

With relief, Kathy recognised where they were. The next bit alongside the river was flat and straight. She wished the effort wouldn't use up all her breath; she'd imagined them running side-by-side and being able to chat a little, and it was all she could do to keep up, even though he said he'd slowed his pace for her. But she was determined: as well as losing some weight and getting into shape, she wanted to be with him. Even though she wasn't an early-morning person.

And there was another benefit: the run was not only energising, but after, it made her feel incredibly sexy. So much so that she might make him late for work again....

The memory made her smile. Things were changing. She was getting an idea of what it took to make a movie. The Americans were turning out to be actually very friendly, and the one called Melanie had given her work as a runner, and said she'd be paid in cash. She did find the pace to be terribly slow sometimes. There seemed to be endless conferring and arguing, and sometimes a scene was shot over again for no reason she could fathom.

Although the longer they took, the better, as far as she was concerned. But Melanie had told her they were unlikely to run over schedule.

The thought sapped Kathy's energy, slowing her down even more. And even though she knew it was petty, she almost stopped, just to test his reaction.

But once the idea of stopping had entered her head, her body followed suit. She found herself at a standstill, and feeling too drained to continue. Angrily, she pulled up the tracksuit bottoms, a perverse part of herself objectively watching the widening gap between them. She waited for him to notice, but Joe just ran on, without once looking back.

The path – an old cinder track at this point – stretched out up the incline in front of her, suddenly daunting. She knew it led back onto the road into town, and guessed he'd stop when he came to the end, do some stretching and walk the last five minutes. Forcing herself into a slow jog, Kathy rehearsed what she might say. She couldn't stand it much longer, the not-knowing what would happen next. Again the round in her head began: how to phrase the question, along with all the possible answers; his point of view as much as her own, a repetitive inner fantasy-dialogue that was beginning to drive her nuts.

If only he would talk about it, she thought petulantly. But he was not a talker. Not shy; it wasn't about that. He just seemed to like silence. And the one time she'd tried to bring the subject of the future up in a joking way, he'd only said he liked to live for the moment, a remark that had made her blood run cold. Now she was too scared to bring up a subject she might regret.

Watching him reach the end of the path and stop, she wished she could see his face when he realised how far behind she'd fallen. But she knew that he never gave anything away. And instead of coming back to see if she was okay, he was using the time to stretch. Feeling her stomach grow heavy and hot, she slowed to a walk. Unable to pick up her leaden feet and run the last bit, she watched the way his black hair fell damp across his face as he stretched his legs and leaned over to massage his thighs and calves through the thin cotton of his tracksuit.

Angrily, she thought how he had never let her give him another massage, since that time in the car. That had helped him, she was sure. Maybe she'd only learned it from a book, but her Mam still often asked for a massage, and guys liked it as well. Although usually as a means to an end. Joe had been no different, that time. Although after, he had been so distant. And it was strange how he wouldn't let her do it again. Well, it was his loss, she decided; she wouldn't ever offer to do it for him again, not now or when they got back or ever.

Aware of the bitter turn her thoughts had taken, Kathy felt sad.

If only it was like back in the beginning, she thought. Time hadn't mattered then. And, despite their special connection, he hadn't noticed that she'd fallen behind and didn't seem to care now he had.

She realised she didn't really know him at all. Oh, she'd found out some things: his age, thanks to a sneaky look at his passport when he'd been in the shower. It had been a bit of a shock. And he wasn't the director of the whole film, just of a unit. The real director was the short, loud show-off with the blonde crew-cut and perpetual baseball cap.

As for his life, trying to extract some information about that had been like trying to prise a limpet off a rock. And once the underbelly was exposed, she'd almost regretted pressing him. Like his having been married, not once, but three times.

A lawyer in New York who had divorced him; some kind of cowgirl, who'd died – it had sounded like cancer – with whom he'd had a daughter he hadn't seen since, a daughter who had to be almost as old as she was. And before them, someone he'd grown up with; there'd been drugs and alcohol, and a car-crash. From the abrupt and broken way he told it, it seemed he had been somehow responsible.

Nor had he given any one of these ex-wives a name, nor even his daughter. And his comments had been stark and cold, as if he didn't care about any one of them in the least any more. It had made him seem heartless, and she'd had the thought that he'd been trying to put her off him.

He'd also mentioned a stint in the army, which was terribly hard for her to imagine, given that the squaddies she'd known were shaven-headed wimps, or thugs.

She knew it was irrational, but coming to know him was taking away some of the magic feeling. As she caught up with Joe, Kathy found herself looking at him with a newly-critical eye, even as she hated herself for doing it. Wearing a black hooded fleece and sweatpants, except for the darkness of his skin and the black pony-tail, she thought he was not really remarkable at all: a middle-aged man trying to keep in shape, with a girl almost half his age in tow. It was almost sort of seedy.

But even now, in this mood, she had to admit it was difficult to tell. He could easily pass for ten years younger. But that didn't change the fact he was almost twice as old as she was.

Yet the way he sometimes talked, that deep and poetic way, made up for the long silences. Even if he didn't think being a red Indian was romantic, she'd never get over it. No-one had ever made her feel anything like he did. She recalled the way he seemed to know exactly what she liked and wanted, how he could bring her to the edge and keep her hovering there till she didn't know where or who she was, then just when she thought she couldn't take any more, tip her over into ecstasy. Even now, just thinking about it, she could recall the sensation, rising with a powerful inevitability from somewhere deep inside her, carrying her out of herself....

"Hey, li'l chickadee, you still with me? Or a thousand miles away?" His voice was soft, as if he sensed something of what was in her head. Kathy looked straight into his dark and patient eyes. She knew this was her chance. Now she could say something about who might soon be a thousand miles away.

But she couldn't get her tongue around the words.

It was like she was racing towards the edge of a cliff, without the faintest idea of how high it was, or what lay beneath.

Student of the sky since childhood, Joe was the one who noticed the intrusion: a long white line drawn across the sky by a jet. He knew it wouldn't take long to disperse; the high-altitude wind was moving more powerfully than the one at ground-level. It was already softening along its edges. After a minor altercation with Jess, a break was called.

The gusting wind, sweeping down across the moors from the north, was needle-sharp cold. Glad of some time free, Joe headed into the tumble of great granite rocks below the ridge, where he found a large hole, freshly interfered with. A spicy sourness hung nearby: fox, he knew. He squatted down to breathe in its wildness, as much as to shelter from the wind.

The sun skulked low and milky in the washed-out sky, forewarning of a change in the weather. But a day of clear skies had brightened everyone's mood, and the chemistry between camera and actor had been at its best.

Joe thought about how casting decisions could ruin a movie, or lead it astray. Owen might be typically British, stiff and formal when he wasn't drinking, but he was well-cast. If only all the actors could realise that for this short time they all inhabited one world, in which no part was too small. A movie had to be a collaborative effort; the director willing to share his vision. If he had one. It was a sad thing, a man who didn't dream.

If he hadn't been clear about it before, Joe now knew for sure why he'd been head-hunted for this movie.

Below him lay a kaleidoscope of tan, grey and green: a checkerboard of ploughed-up land, pasture, dark woods. The thought of a smoke crossed his mind, but he was beginning to realise that he was close to feeling content. His first lady, mary-jane, had lost her prime place in his life. For the moment, anyway.

Kathy. Joe mouthed her name, thought about her natural grace, her good manners, her serious, watchful face. He remembered the way her body received him, welcoming, always ready, and felt a

warming response in his own. Closing his eyes, he recalled her on
the bed, face down, arms spread-eagled; the line of her body rising
to the curve of her buttocks; the sheen of sweat in the small of her
back; the fine blonde hairs glistening on the back of her strong
thighs and the cleft of her ass. The way she'd raised her rump to
meet him; the soft cushion of it against him, her curving spine and
hands clutching at the pillow.... His groin throbbed heavily with
remembered pleasure.

She thought he didn't look at her, but he knew every part of her,
intimately. She was mapped out in his mind: smooth limbs and
belly; curve of her hip; flare of her collar-bone; soft hollow at her
throat. It was a kind of high in itself, he knew, a girl so young and
attractive, and so infatuated. But on her part, knowing their time
together was finite had to be part of the attraction; she lived in a
fairy-tale world where relationships were concerned.

Joe hadn't wanted to speak of it, but had felt he had to give
something in return for her genuine openness. And in the telling of
his past, he'd recognised his own motive: he'd imagined the
blinkers of infatuation would lift from her eyes and she'd see him
clearly as just another weak, fault-filled human being.

How he'd become the pet project of a civil-rights lawyer who'd
married him and spirited him off to live in New York, shaping him
and bringing him to work that he could love, then dropping him
when a more needy case had come along. It had brought out a
residual anger, and he'd found himself pushing the girl away in the
telling, afraid he might lash out. But she hadn't been angry back at
him, or jealous; she'd been the wise one, pointing out how people
might help each other through a stage in their lives: it was because
of Jay he'd gone to film school.

She had actually compared her to Mary Poppins.

Even now, the image of beautiful Jay, her luxurious bright blond
hair in a severe bun, wearing a matronly black governess's dress
and carrying a little black umbrella, floating away through the air
with her feet splayed like Charlie Chaplin's, made him smile.

At the time, he'd laughed out loud: great bursts of laughter, heaving from his belly. After, he'd felt peaceful about her for the first time in years.

As for Lindy, the space she occupied was cauterised. Or so he'd thought until he'd flashed back on how she'd wasted away, so fast. Little Evie's large, dark eyes and wan little face, haloed by a black tumble of curls, had come flooding back on a tide of guilt.

Evie's birth had been the day that his life had seemed to begin to change. Like a coming-out: all the elements of the world placed afresh with the placing of the child into his arms; living and non-living, past and future, the spirit of animals, plants, wind, time, the stars. With the birth, the web that is the inner pattern of all things was made again. All things were in balance, and his world was made steady. And then it had all fallen apart.

Kathy hadn't asked for details, nor did she act judgemental when he found himself admitting he'd been too drunk to care for his daughter; too drunk to care at all, about any of it.

"Part of you died then, too. Don't judge yourself with your mind, look into your heart."

Those were her wise words, the little English. It was the sort of thing he'd say when he was in the mood to charm a woman into bed, and had pulled him up short. Sometimes, things happened like that with her: the mask slipped, and she acted like a mirror.

And Annie. Her name hadn't crossed his lips for a couple of decades and probably never would, yet he'd spoken of that deep, hidden anguish. Already heading off-track when they married, too young, he'd refused to move in with her clan, upsetting everyone deeply, and things had spiralled downhill from then on. Liquor had ruled him, and to this day, he couldn't remember how it had happened: the pick-up upside down in the gully, her broken body, the blood seeping into the dust of the roadside.

That was the first time he had seen it, the turning of a wheel, round and round, as he realised his own parents' legacy. Even the colour of the pick-up had been the same. The only difference was that he, Joe, had survived. Was that the breaking of the pattern?

Somehow, he thought, this English girl drew him from himself, squeezed words from him like water from a stone. Deep and dark, the pools of memory lay at his feet, and he saw again how it was as if he drew destruction to those he might allow himself to get close to. He couldn't allow it to happen again.

But he was nearly done here, the shooting almost completed. And it was just as well; the girl unsettled him. He'd believed he'd understood what was happening: his exoticism answering her need for adventure; her youth, her bright energy speaking to his own need. A fair exchange. And through no fault of his own, it had a limited life-span. In a way, they were kind of equals: equal in what they gave, or took. And he had to admit, knowing she was waiting for him at the end of the day had added something intangible to the shape of it. Only she seemed somehow to have intruded. It was as if she were in him. Like he was infected with a ghost-sickness, something he remembered the old folk speaking of.

Aware of his obsessive personality, Joe realised it was as if his boundaries were expanding, affecting the way he saw things. The making of the movie seemed to have taken on a clearer meaning and greater significance; and when Jess showed himself, such as when he criticised others for his own failings, he realised that it barely touched him. Watching the girl's natural, quick and friendly response to people, even people she might never see again, he saw how he could learn to become more considerate of the people he worked with. The crew were probably quite human, if he allowed himself to get to know them.

Her English way of talking appealed to him; the soft, lilting accent. And he liked that she had an inner world: she read books, wrote poetry. Or so she said. She didn't offer to show them to him, or repeat any of them. But she had a way with words. Her whisperings when they made love could move him to a whole other level, where he was both less and more himself. Although that time in the car, when everything had spun out of control, had filled him with panic. Since then, he'd been more careful.

But he knew she'd sensed his retreat; that was why she became resentful occasionally. And truth be told, he felt resentful too. His old way of being was becoming drained of meaning; but if he let go, allowed any feelings, they'd only be injured.

Yet it was in his power to make his life a more meaningful, harmonious one.

Was this why he had been sent to this cold northern island, thousands of miles from his roots: to help shape a timeless love-story, while living a new one himself?

He realised he was being moved into the realm of feelings, dreams and memory. And it was the place he was most afraid of, because it was haunted by the dead. They walked there, spoke to him there. The losses in his life had overwhelmed him; he had cut and run. His life had become one of avoidance. He'd retreated and stayed there: in his mind, where the pain in his heart couldn't reach.

The ache in his side made Joe straighten up and stretch. So absorbed in himself was he, that he didn't realise Ray had appeared above him on top of the rock, and only just managed to cover the fact that he'd been taken by surprise.

"Hey, Joe, if you're back with us on planet earth, we'd appreciate your co-operation," Ray laughed. "We're movin' the whole shot a hunnerd yards down the slope. That way the ridge'll screen what's left of the contrail."

As he emerged from the shelter of the rocks, the frigid wind bit into Joe's skin with teeth like sharp glass. Stamping his feet back into life, he blew into his fists to warm them and caught the fecund sea-smell of her on his fingers. Filling his lungs with her aroma and the cold air, he let his gaze sweep across the rock-tattooed, sheep-strewn, craggy moors. In the distance lay the massive, snow-dusted hump of the Cheviot, like a beached whale.

It was a desolate, lonely land, the few trees gnarled and wind-bent, but under the earth, there was a sense of new life, stirring. Reminded somehow of the arid, high-country Mars-scape of his childhood, his youth, a powerful upsweep of emotion suffused Joe's body. Then out of the blue, a terrifying thought struck him: "I could live here."

FIVE

Massed, hulking clouds blot up the sun; the horizon is lost in a gauze of fog. Dull and leaden, the sea laps at the shore with a slick tongue. Oyster-catchers ebb and flow at the water's edge, moving as a unit with the surf. Above, high atop the dunes, dark and brooding, looms the great fortress of Bamburgh.

On the strand are four heavy war-horses, dark of mane and body, and wearing simple trappings. They snort and shake their magnificent heads, rattling their bridles. Great feathered hooves stamp, kicking up fine sprays of white sand.

The riders are all of a type: broad and bearded, wearing leather boots and dark cloaks. Gesticulating and exchanging loud words, they tug at the reins and kick at their mounts' withers, turning the horses in tight, skittish circles. One of the riders, cloaked in night-blue, his dark hair elaborately braided, pulls out his sword and brandishes it in the air, causing his mount to rear. At one with the beast, he leans into its neck, and when it calms, sweeps his sword-arm in a wide arc.

"Two more turns is all I ask."

Amplified by the damp air, his words carry clearly. Then, standing up in his stirrups, he calls out a strange word, loudly.

His voice signals cohesive action. Fair hair flowing free, his black cloak decorated with a red rune, another of the knights is clearly impatient to leave. He whoops excitedly and with a kick at his horse's flanks, thunders away down the strand, closely followed by another of the riders. Flying clods of sand are hurled up behind them.

As one, the sea-birds take flight, swooping low over the water with piercing, mournful cries.

From among the dunes appears a lone figure, riding side-saddle on a graceful white horse. Red-gold hair a fiery stream behind her, green cloak flapping wildly, she gallops down towards the two remaining knights. The waiting horses whicker in recognition.

Guinevere comes to a prancing stop beside them, struggling to control her mount. Sides heaving, the mare steps sideways, a wild-eyed coquette tossing her head, as her rider speaks quietly but agitatedly to Lancelot. Her face is flushed with cold and wet with tears.

"There came a dream, and in it, he spoke to me. All has come clear now. This time that lay between has made my heart to see. There was nothing but my mind that stood between you and me.... But it is too late, my lord; much, much too late. I am to devote what is left of my sorry life."

The knight manoeuvres his horse alongside hers and grasps the mare's bridle. Guinevere falls silent as they come face-to-face. Breaths mingling, they stare at each other, searchingly, for a long moment, then she kicks at her horse, who jerks away, forcing Lancelot to let go. In one smooth movement she turns her mount and gallops back in the direction from which she has come, her cloak an emerald-green swirl in her wake.

Hooves digging deep in the sand for purchase, the two war-horses prance and plunge, as if anxious to be after the white mare. Pulling sharply on the reins, their riders bring them under control, then almost as one, they lash their mounts' necks with flying reins and storm off along the shore in the opposite direction.

Seams of sunlight open in the dark and heavy clouds. A lancing shaft floods the great fortress with a soft, silver-gold light.

Previously unseen, a dark, stooped figure cautiously emerges from its hidden place among the grey rocks at the water's edge, its cloak a ragged robe hanging from bent shoulders, its face invisible under the hood. Looking more like an ancient, bedraggled crow than a human being, it stares after the direction Guinevere has taken, then advances to where the meeting took place. Crouching low, it appears to pick up something from one of the scuffed hoof-prints.

Or maybe it barely brushes the sand with a palm, before hobbling off in the direction the queen has taken.

They'd wrapped up early for the day; it wasn't dark yet. Kathy felt agitated, although she had no idea why.

"Let's do something special." She pushed at Joe's arm, even though she knew he didn't like being touched while driving.

"The way the sun hit the castle, just at that moment...." A note of wonder coloured Joe's voice. "Had a hunch to keep a camera on it. And the little birds, the way they moved.... Like they was a single organism. Or one of 'em was leader an' his thought ran through the whole flock. Or did they all have the same thought at the same time?"

"Who cares? I'm sick of the stupid movie. That's all we ever do: freeze our bums off, hanging around, talking movie, movie, movie; then back to the hotel-room.... Like I said, let's do something; let's go somewhere different; we've got time. After all, tomorrow's the last day we'll have ... this might be the only chance...." Kathy hesitated, uneasy about bringing up the subject and throwing out such unsubtle hints, and glanced at him.

His expression gave nothing away, as usual.

How he could always keep so still and unmoved, even when Jess was throwing a fit and yelling or one of the primes was having a tantrum, was beyond her. Disgruntled, she thought about how he never reacted. She wanted to provoke him into telling her how he really felt about her, or what he thought would happen next, but wasn't sure she'd like what she would hear.

Joe drove on. Glumly looking ahead at the narrow road, Kathy gripped the sides of her seat, feeling the silence between them pressing on her, heavy as a wet blanket. Eventually, she decided to take things in hand. Wracking her brain, she tried to think of what lay between where they now were, and town.

"Take the next road on the left," she instructed.

Without a word, he did so. The atmosphere in the car seemed to be growing thicker. After she gave him the next direction, she began to regret her earlier outburst. She'd promised herself she'd stay calm and quiet and appreciative. Instead, she was making stupid, petty demands, like she wanted to go out on a date. He wasn't that kind of man, and she wasn't a teenager any more. She realised that the trembling, hollow feeling in her tummy wasn't from hunger.

The gorse bushes lining the roadside hampered the view, but an occasional glimpse of the sea reassured her that they'd come the right way. Recognising the sharp curve to the right, she told him to park on the grass verge.

Joe turned off the engine and sat looking out the window, hands on the wheel, saying nothing. Deciding she could play this game too, she ignored him and got out.

The wind had picked up and the clouds were breaking apart. Without checking to see what Joe was doing, Kathy pulled her hood over her head and strode off down the grassy lane towards the sea. Bordered on both sides by a formidable gauntlet of barbed wire and clumps of gorse, it led to an old iron kissing-gate. Passing through it, she surreptitiously checked. He was several feet behind her. Hardening herself – and hating this part of her which seemed to have taken over but unable to stop it – she barely glanced at the stone cottage, empty for years, on the top of an escarpment to her left, a place she'd often fantasised about living in, and walked swiftly down a narrow sandy path cut deep into the grass, to the sliver of beach.

Suddenly what she was doing took on an edge: taking him to one of the places she most loved, a monument to the power of wind and sea, a citadel of natural stone sculptures, carved by the forces of nature over thousands of years. A dark and moody place, where she came sometimes – all too rarely – to be on her own. But she knew this would be like in miniature, compared to what he grew up with, and not at all impressive to him.

Finding the familiar, worn footholds, she easily scaled the low sandstone cliff that acted as a sort of natural barrier. Once over the top, she saw that the tide was almost full.

Somehow, nothing mattered quite so much any more.

The timing was perfect: with such a heavy swell, she knew the spout would be blowing. Forgetting herself for a moment, Kathy scrambled over reams of pastel-coloured sandstone, networked with cracks and protruding seams and bowl-shaped pools, to the edge of a great aperture, wide as a swimming-pool and at least twice as deep. Inside, the murky water seethed angrily. She waited.

Eventually, the waters sucked back mightily and began to heave upwards again. There was a gurgling and a hissing, and from a hidden place in the rocks on the far side, a jet of water shot high into the air and across to where she was standing, to be followed by another defiant spurt which didn't quite make it. Licking the briny taste from her cheek, Kathy felt the same thrill as the first time she'd come here and seen the forces of nature at work. Hoping Joe had seen it too, she glanced over her shoulder.

He was standing just behind her, his face inscrutable, his eyes narrowed against the cold east wind. But he nodded his head, once, slowly, and Kathy knew that he knew.

"It's called Rumbling Kern," she said proudly.

"Kern?"

"Don't know. Maybe something to do with corner, or hinge. Like there's another world just the other side of it, you know?"

She looked back into the great, gaping hole in the rocks, where the waters roiled, rising and falling like the breathing of a trapped and maddened monster. To her, it was like the entrance to the netherworld of the ocean, to Neptune's lair. When she was younger, she'd used to imagine a mermaid rising slowly to the surface to take a guarded look at the world of air, her hair spread around her like the bands of kelp that swayed seductively in the depths.

All around, ramparts of rock rose like castle walls. On the far side, beyond the spout-hole, stood an imposing tower, whittled out of the sandstone by wind and sea, and crowned with grass.

A loud gurgling, slapping sound heralded another spout of water, which arced even higher. With a laugh, Kathy danced away from the heavy drops that rained down around them, and as the waters sucked back, she pointed silently out to the open sea just beyond, to a section of rock shaped like a low wall which emerged, dark with seaweed and running with little waterfalls.

As she'd anticipated, the next swell that broke against it created a mighty fan of spray that flared silver and white, before the greater waters surged over it again.

Beyond, in the distance, yet another of the monuments on this castle-crowned coastline was just visible: a long, grey shape of broken battlements, almost indistinguishable from the land to the unknowing eye.

She knew then where they would spend the next day; their only whole day together. The last one. Her excitement edged with sadness, Kathy waited for Joe to say something, or at least make some sign of appreciation. Nodding hardly did justice to her most favourite place in all the world; all the more precious because she'd told no-one, and hardly ever came here since it was hard to get to without a car. She looked at him, looking at the sea.

It wasn't the first time she'd noticed how the outer edges of his almond-shaped eyes were laced with tiny wrinkles, but now it was as if she were seeing him with different eyes, as if his real age were suddenly exposed. His coat blew open, and the silver belt-buckle with the geometric design and turquoise stone in the middle that she'd admired now looked ostentatious and flashy. The tight feeling in her chest became almost too much to bear, and she turned to face him.

"Well, so, is that it?" she burst out.

He frowned, the line between his eyes biting deep.

Kathy's mouth was dry. She licked her lips and waited, then out it came: "Happy you got what you wanted? Free shags for the week?"

Part of her was curling up inside in dismay. Even though the thought had crossed her mind, she'd no intention to say it. But now she'd started, she couldn't stop. "What d'you Americans call it ... an easy lay?"

Seeing him wince, she knew she'd scored. Part of her felt vilified, a hard and gleeful part; while another, softer, deeper part wailed at the irreversible damage she was inflicting.

"Thought you didn't much care for words like that." His voice neutral, Joe raised his eyebrows in a sort of mild surprise.

Scarcely able to believe that was all he could say, Kathy felt her stomach give a lurch. What was wrong with him? Couldn't he give as good as he got?

"Oh, what the fuck do I care? Fuck, shag. They're just words. Good old Anglo-Saxon words." Although she actually disliked these words coming out of her mouth, and part of her could hardly believe she was doing this, she had to go on: "And that was all you wanted, wasn't it? You fancy yourself as some kind of ... of sugar-daddy!"

She thought he looked guilty, and felt vindicated. She'd hit the nail on the head. Trembling with the force of her emotions, which were more mixed than she knew, she waited for him to say something, anything, as long as it had some feeling. She waited and waited, then could wait no more. "D'you think I'm that kind of girl? I've never done anything like this before!"

Again that frown. "Why here?"

"Now you expect to do it here? That I brought you here for a shag?" Her voice didn't even sound like hers; it was high and screechy.

Joe shook his head, closed his eyes. "Why do this here? This beautiful place you brought me to ... why bring such anger here?"

With a sinking feeling, Kathy knew he was right, but she had to go on. "Just tell me what you feel for me. I've told you. What about you? What do you feel? I can't believe you feel nothing at all...."

Joe looked away again, out to sea, and Kathy felt a twisting stab between her breasts and a sickly feeling spreading up into her throat and down into her stomach. She'd spoiled it all, and she didn't know why.

When he eventually spoke, his voice was low. "I think I understand why you brought me here."

Her blood thundering in her ears, loud as the sea pounding on the rocks, she couldn't stand that, either. "Don't patronise me. Say what you feel."

Shaking his head gently, Joe shrugged and looked up into the sky.

Kathy looked up, following his gaze. The first star was twinkling: a cold, hard diamond in a gap among the greyness, in a patch of darkening blue. Glancing back at him, as if for the first time, she saw him clearly: a lonely man with a terrible history, with no-one in his life right now but her. Strands of hair had escaped his pony-tail; as he pushed them away from his face, she looked at his hand, the smoothness of the skin, the darker knuckles, the small white triangular scar just below his wrist, and remembered what that hand had done for her, to her.

She could almost feel the sadness in him. The hardness inside her began to melt. How could she be so mean, so nasty, so unfair? Flooded with contrition, Kathy reached out her hand and took hold of his wrist.

"Oh, Joe," she said, feeling like her heart would break. "I'm so sorry. I don't know what came over me. I didn't mean to ... if I could take it back, I would. I know you work hard and you've got a lot on your mind, while I sit around doing hardly anything all day. It's just that being on my own so much gets me thinking about, you know, things, and I should just be happy to be with you. And I am.... I'm so sorry." Tears pricked at her eyes, and she looked up at his face.

He made no move, nor took his gaze from the sky. She squeezed his arm to emphasise her apology, then moved closer, put her arms round him and laid her head against his chest.

But for the thud of his heart and the warmth coming through the material, he might have been a stone statue.

It's over, she thought, and I was the one who spoiled it. Nan was right about my big mouth.

Then she felt his hand touch the top of her head, lightly, and his other arm round her shoulders, cradling her.

"Hey, li'l chickadee." His voice was soft, and calm. "It's past 'n' gone, just like a squall on the ocean."

Hearing the familiar pet-name, Kathy felt like it wasn't quite the end of the world. "Oh, Joe, I love you so much I can't bear it."

Breathing in the musky scent of him, she hugged him, hard. A hiccup jerked her chest, and she felt him tighten his hold on her. Desperately wanting to make it up to him, to wipe it away totally, she pressed her body against his. She wanted to wash away the pain, the ugliness she'd just created; make him forget she'd ever spoken.

"I'm so sorry. I don't know what came over me," she whispered, touching him intimately. "I'll show you how much I care."

"You don't have to."

"I want to." The only problem was, he wasn't responding.

See, you've really gone and done it, a little voice crowed inside Kathy's head. It's over. He'll dump you now, and it's all your own fault.

Standing in the shower, letting the steam build up, Joe considered how she'd turned on him. It hadn't taken long. If only she wouldn't make demands, he thought, but gave him time to work things out. Women were all the same: once past the infatuation, they wanted control. Then came the inevitable: how he had to change. What started out as a diversion, a bit of fun, took on a serious note. Demands were made. They always wanted to know how he felt. And what the future held, as if he were some kind of seer. But he knew well enough that whenever he plotted out a future, life had a way of pulling the rug out from under his feet, painfully. He'd long ago learned to take things a day at a time and not give his word on anything.

An outburst like that would normally have marked the time for him to move on. But that was about to happen in any case. Except, he was realising, he didn't want this one to just slip away from him.

The thought struck Joe like a fist: he hadn't allowed it into his mind so completely before.

What had happened? He'd only meant to enjoy some female company for a few days, made simple by the clear-cut "out" at the end, when they returned to London; and, after that Los Angeles, to work on the rushes....

Then what? He'd be walking away alone, into an unknown, featureless future. Not an unfamiliar scene by any means, one that had never touched him before, but now, something about it made him feel even more tired. Yet what could he do? He had nothing to offer.

A rundown old trailer, way back in the boonies, back in his own rootland, was where he was headed after this. Standpipe, no power, no phone line; the place probably taken over by vermin by now and needing work. A beat-up old Ford Mustang. And maybe he was okay for a while, but he had no idea when work would come his way again.

The girl's roots were here. This was her land. She was simply at the age to leave this little town, which she said she'd been wanting to do anyway, and look for the brighter lights of the city, where more would happen for her. She was intelligent and educated enough to find herself some work pretty quick.

That had to be it, he decided. The typical yearning of the young, imagining there was always something better over the horizon. She had to learn, like all the rest. But better for her to learn in the place where she belonged. It struck him to give her some money, so she'd get herself a head-start. If she would take it; she had pride, and dignity. To save her face, he'd never told her that what she'd earned as a runner had been his idea, paid for out of his own pocket.

Yet the thought of her carrying on with her life, maybe remembering him from time to time until he faded into oblivion when another guy took his place, made Joe feel strangely one-dimensional. For a moment, he tried to imagine coming back north for a while after London, seeing what happened. But he knew that was unrealistic. He had no wish to meet any of her family. Their prejudice had already been made clear. There was nothing for him, here.

Wrapping a towel around himself, he walked back into the room to find her lying on the bed, still with all her clothes on. That was a first, but he wasn't surprised. Not responding to her when she'd been so sorry had been unfair, but he couldn't help it, his body had gone numb and stayed that way. He felt he had to try and to find a way to make it up to her; it was not good to leave with sourness in his wake.

"Hey, English," he said, combing through his hair with his fingers. "I'll order us a picnic for tomorrow an' we'll go follow that coast trail you talked about, okay?" He felt awkward; he'd never cared to seek approval before.

Kathy sat up and looked at him searchingly. He wished he could see how she saw him.

"Oh, Joe, that's fantastic. Exactly what I'd been hoping for: a day for just the two of us." She got up and came to him. Easily and naturally she flowed into his arms and, suddenly dizzy, he had a sense of the room tipping and her body being the only solid thing to cling to. He closed his eyes, rested his chin on the top of her head and rocked her gently.

How had he let it come to this, allowing his painfully-won barriers to be breached? He was creaking into middle age, classically trying to capture a lost youth. Or maybe just doing his bit for race relationships.... He smiled, a small private smile, thinking of the races warring within himself.

Yet when he tried to imagine not having her round ... it wasn't just the sex, or the companionship. She'd shown him something about himself. He'd noticed the way he'd slipped back in a more natural way of talking. It was like the part of him he'd been careful to keep under wraps was resurfacing. Or a sense that something greater than himself was living through him. The thought of turning his back on it made him feel physically sick.

But he had no idea what he could do about it, and fear kept him silent.

Muffled by the sea-fret, pebbles clucked in the ebb-tide, which swelled and unravelled in soft, feathery surges. A rift in the dewy mist that enveloped the high-cliffed promontory revealed a serrated sea dull as pewter, which might have been a hundred or several thousand feet below them.

Her back against Joe, nestled into the comforting warm bulk of his body, contained in his coat and arms, Kathy could pretend they were on some kind of spaceship. Flying away, free. Just like in the fairy-tale, he had cut his way through the briars, defeated the dragon and kissed her awake. She felt completely at peace, as if this moment was what her life had been about: to bring her to the ruins of Dunstanburgh castle, to a broken tower on the high edge of the land, another of her most favourite places in the world, to be at one with this man of another race, another culture, another continent.

She thought about asking him to play his flute again. It would somehow seal the magic. But he never had, since that first time. Once, when she'd asked, he'd said something about how it didn't work like that.

"That rhythm...." Joe said softly.

Her back pressed to his chest, Kathy could feel the vibration of his voice, and it thrilled her as much as it had in the beginning.

"Like in the womb," he continued. "Swish of blood, movin' through the veins of the Mother, whispering of early creation. Oldest, widest womb.... There'll come a time when she'll groan an' howl an' beat herself against the land. Through the labour of the Mother, comes all life...."

Kathy felt warmth blossom in her chest. When he talked like

this, it was like he was letting her into the most secret heart of himself. Today, this special and perfect day, the only whole day on their own together, he was himself. She'd never been so happy; all she had to do was keep the thought of it being their last day out of her mind.

But as soon as she'd thought it, it sat there, squat as a toad, heavy and cold as wet snow, demanding her attention.

"You won't forget me, will you?" She bit into her cheek, hating herself for how she would think about something, resolve not to say anything about it, yet out it came, regardless. "Oh, effing.... I didn't mean to say that. It just sort of came out, like."

After several moments, he squeezed her to him. "I remember how the old folk, if someone did somethin' outta character, somethin' no-one could understand why they did it, they'd say, 'A dark wind moved through him', and sorta look the other way."

A shiver ran down Kathy's spine. She imagined a shadowy wraith, sliding into a body, taking possession and sparking some horrible action. Then she remembered something he'd once said.

"But what if someone did something really awful? Like ... kill someone?" She could hardly believe she was doing it again. Why couldn't she keep her mouth shut?

"It's a disruption in the pattern, the ultimate evil, to take a human life. But in the old times, there wasn't punishment as we know it now. The old way was gifts of compensation to the family, an' initiation into the proper medicine society to be cured, to restore harmony to the self. There'd be a sing. The whole village'd come out, for days..."

"To sing?" Kathy frowned, finding it hard to imagine. "I can't see how that would ever work, certainly not nowadays."

"To discipline using fear don't work. Doin' time don't, neither."

From the tone of his voice, Kathy was aware of a certain bitterness. She wanted to ask if it was from personal experience, but it felt like she was always the nosy one.

"Can't imagine a 'dark wind' plea working nowadays. Can you imagine, a choir in the courts...?" She spoke as lightly as she could and was gratified when he laughed.

"You're good for me, li'l chickadee." He traced a line down her cheek with one gentle finger, circled it under her chin and turned her face up to his.

Looking into the velvety darkness of his eyes, Kathy felt a responding warmth blossom in her stomach. It flowed up into her chest and throat, and downwards, lava-like, into her thighs, making her knees go weak. When he kissed her, gently and expressively, she felt she would have melted onto the rough grass, had he not been holding her so tight.

"This place," he said when they drew apart again, "has a special kinda buzz. Can feel it through the soles of my feet. If I'd've known 'bout this place, I'd've pushed for some shots here."

Barely back into herself, Kathy said, "But it's Bamburgh that was connected to Lancelot."

"This one's got somethin'... a feeling, of great mystery.... Like that old magician Merlin cast one of his spells here, an' it's still at work. Who knows, maybe we're not on the ground at all an' the buzz I'm feelin' is from motorin' along, like in an airship. Who can tell, a day like this, when you can't see the land, can't see where this fog ends an' where the sky begins. Puts me in mind of how I get when we.... Maybe you're a part of the enchantment."

Say it! a demonic little voice clamoured in Kathy's head. This time she kept her mouth under control.

"I was thinking that, before," she said eventually. "That we were on some kind of a spaceship, I mean. Funny how we often have the same thought. There's a legend about this place: something about a princess being held prisoner. Or maybe it was a dragon, I don't remember. And a seven-fold task for the prince to set her, or it, free. But who'd want to set a dragon free? Wish I could remember stories like you do."

"Your land's steeped in legend. I had to go to the old story-tellers. You'll learn, just like I did, despite everything.... But this land of yours, it's got a raw, powerful energy." Joe's voice changed, and he added, so quietly she could barely hear him, "Sometimes, it's like I know it."

Although their position didn't change, Kathy could feel him sort of moving away from her again. It wasn't physical; but she could tell by the way he was breathing that he was thinking deeply. After a while, however, he seemed to snap out of it.

"The point of the stories, the myths," he continued. "Well, they're like symbols. Not what they seem on the surface. Like your parables. You gotta peel back the layers-"

"Just like getting to know a person!" Kathy felt jubilant, making the connection. "Maybe that's all we are, people I mean: symbols ... for life!" She laughed, liking what had to be one of the best things she'd ever come up with. "So that's why we create things, build things, 'cause we're building life."

Joe hesitated, then swept one arm in an arc. "So then, what does all this serve? And you 'n' me; what's the point?"

Kathy didn't know how to answer that, so she stayed silent. Then she realised it was the first time he'd put them together in this way: "you and me". But even though it seemed like he might be beginning to think of them as a couple, she felt somehow helpless, useless and ignorant. She had a feeling that the answer might be the most important thing she might ever come up with; that it would be the thing that would keep them together.

Joe's voice seemed to come from far away. "The beauty way, that's what it serves. A person is in the world to live in it, not change it."

His words resounded in Kathy's head. It was perfect, even if she had no idea what he meant.

Joe let Kathy do what she wanted. Lying back, he accepted her mouth, her tongue, on his body. She might not know it, but she was more adept when she hadn't been drinking. She was more sensitive, varying sensation and pace. Hands cupped behind his head, he allowed himself to take pleasure in the glistening, hanging fall and spread of her hair, the way it glinted in the candlelight, the silken feel of it, sliding across his thighs. When she began to apply more pressured stimulation, he guessed she was trying to bring him to climax. But such coercion only buried his release even deeper.

After a few minutes, she let him go. But only momentarily. Sitting up on her knees, she straddled him, flicked back her hair and swooped down on him like a bird of prey, snatching him up inside her. He could see she had to have her way with him, and let her dictate the frenetic plunging and thrusting. It was like some kind of assault; under his hands, her hips and back became damp with sweat. Joe thought he should make some appreciative noise, but the bed was beginning to creak loudly, as if it might not withstand the stress.

"Ain't my ol' bones," he found himself saying. "Had a good lube job, earlier."

She stopped moving so suddenly, it was almost a shock. Then she laughed, and fell over sideways, taking him with her.

"Bet they never heard anything like this since the Vikings landed," she gasped. "Well, it'll give them something to fantasise about, until the next invasion. In the summer; tourists, I mean."

Joe chuckled, then found himself laughing with her as they came apart. He hadn't given a thought to the paper-thin walls of the place they'd found, the small, quaint cottage, a "B&B", as it was known, in a fishing-village. Laughter rolled back and forth between them, and ebbed away. He heard her sigh.

Moving over her, he insinuated himself again between her thighs and in one smooth movement gathered her to him and rolled back on his side. She flowed with him, one of her legs bent under him, in the hollow of his waist, and the other hooked over his hip. Deftly, he slid back inside her, sealing the moment with a long kiss, keeping his body still now but for the gentle teasing at her lips, the suggestion of his tongue. Her taste was salty-sweet; just like smell and taste of her body.

Then even the playing at the mouth he stopped and, confident of himself within her, kept quite still, knowing the stillness would bring the more subtle sensations back to life in her; would return her to the full knowledge of him, buried in her body.

Feeling the slight, sweet embrace within her depths, he knew he was beginning to take effect. With one finger, his ring-finger, he traced the delicate moulding of her throat, enjoying the soft light of the candle – her idea – the way it licked at the shadows. Her eyes still closed, she sighed again.

Joe adjusted his breathing to match hers. Watching her face, he feather-touched the vein on her neck that he knew to be especially sensitive, noting the trembling of her eyelids, the tightening of her lips. He used his fingertips to brush her throat.

It never ceased to amaze him: the sensitivity of the most vulnerable areas. Jay had taught him well.

Unusually, the intrusive thought of the woman who had caused him so much pain did not disturb him. Kissing Kathy softly, he slid his hand down over the curves of breast, waist, hip, and clasped her buttocks, holding her to him as he moved deeper into her. He felt a tightening around him down there, a gentle squeezing. The sensation was tender, caring. Spontaneously moving again in response, he had to close his eyes. For a long and delicious while, they continued in this way, kissing and rocking, until, opening his eyes again, he looked straight into Kathy's.

Her eyes were storm-blue and strangely luminous, the pupils dilated; her expression one of yearning. He felt her hand move down the back of his thigh, and the sensitivity of the skin behind his knee as she stroked it surprised him, sending a rush up his back. She moved on, sliding her hand up his outer leg to his hip, where it cupped the jut of the pelvic-bone, held it as if owning it.... Then it travelled on to his waist, fingertips trailing around and over his belly and the contours of his chest.

It was as if she were painting his body. And as she stroked his upper chest and throat, Joe had to close his eyes. The fiery sensation in the wake of her touch reached back down into his groin, making him swell warm and heavy.

Her other hand joined in. She cradled his neck, and he felt her thumb touch the lobe of his ear, gently trace its outline.

"The candle is a symbol of my love." Her voice was almost an intrusion, but Joe went along with it. "A single flame, like the love in which we two burn as one."

She moved against him, kissing him lightly, then whispered against his mouth: "With this kiss, we are of one breath. And with this...."

Joe felt a sweet, rippling sensation, embracing him, taking him deeper into her.

"The flame of my passion. We are one desire." She pressed her hand over his heart. "We are one heart, one love. Joe, I love you."

The words were beautiful and echoed in his mind. For a moment, he let himself feel her. Not just her body, but who and what she was.

As if carried on his breathing, or on an inner current that sprang from deep within him, Joe felt his body begin to move. The beginnings of the timeless dance. Like a great, swelling wave, he rose to meet her, and felt her adjust, accept, move as one with him. There was an ebbing, and, as he gripped her buttocks in both his hands, again the surge rose in him, into her. Together they rode the billowing wave.

And almost he gave a whoop, but it was she who sounded their pleasure: a soft, drawn-out moan. As the feeling began to recede, their mouths touched gently. And again the great surge took him; transported them.

Overcome by the power of the feelings, Joe found he couldn't track them or plot what should come next. He had no choice but to let go and allow them their rhythm: the flowing and the ebbing. An effortless, compelling natural force that silenced the voice in his head and swept the two of them along together, in an everlasting, swaying, undulating embrace.

How long they continued in this way, he would never know. Eventually, like a wind-ruffle across the ocean, approached a change of some kind. Barely had he registered the sharp ripple that engulfed his groin and ran the length of him, when a great tidal wave of sensation prickled madly throughout his groin and stomach and down into his legs and feet and flooded his chest, and he felt himself lifted. The wind threw the sea up against the sky; her small, bird-like cry was lost in the storm. In dizzy confusion, he almost let the words come out: I love you. But the breath was snatched from his mouth and his mind from his head, as the tumultuous, throbbing release engulfed him. Out of himself but for the sweet pulsing in his groin, floating, transcendent....

As if in a dream-state, he heard it again in his heart: Kathy, I love you.

Joe took a deep and shuddering breath. The backwash of his orgasm was turning his limbs soft, like molten metal. He could feel his heart drumming in his chest, and a sense of wonder filled him as he realised the beauty of what had just happened. Not only he, out of control, spontaneous; but she, too. For that timeless time, they had truly been as one.

For a fleeting moment, Joe became aware of her as not just a girl, but a woman: fully a woman, and a wise woman at that. And while the feeling of being naked and helpless and weak as a baby scared him, underneath he could also sense something that was entirely new to him, and difficult to put a name to at first.

It was joy.

Holding Kathy close to him, feeling her pulse still racing, as was his own, he heard her murmur sleepily: "I love you."

Knowing how much she wanted him to echo her, he waited. To his relief, he felt her slipping away, as she jerked suddenly and grew heavy in his arms.

Low, scudding clouds raced across the sky, releasing stinging slaps of icy rain. The seagulls mewled and whined, riding the wind above their heads like harbingers of doom. Kathy wished they would go off and pester someone else for food, but there was no-one to be seen anywhere.

Which was hardly surprising, she thought. Only fools and madmen would come out in this sort of weather. North-east wind, fit to freeze a fox.

The rain was beginning to turn to sleet. She threw her last crust into the air for one of the plucky birds to catch, and turned to Joe. "Race you back to the car!" Taking off at full speed, she knew that if she kept the advantage of surprise, she might beat him.

As usual, he'd neglected to lock it. She pulled open the door and jumped inside, laughing as he arrived moments behind her.

"The man I love may have hair coal-black; but when we race, it's speed he lacks!" she quipped. "God, now that was pathetic!"

Sitting himself behind the wheel, Joe winked at her. "She's white as snow; always ready to go." He shook his head. "Now that don't quite hit the spot, neither."

Kathy waited to see if he would find something better, then quietly asked: "So what would?"

"Huh?"

Exasperated, she knew it was no use to press it. He'd heard her, but he wasn't going to deal with it. She suddenly felt like she could throttle him.

"Kathy...."

For a wonderful moment, she thought she might be wrong.

"Help me out here, wouldja? Seems I lost the keys." Joe was twisting in his seat and rummaging in his pockets; he emptied them, one by one, onto the dashboard: his wallet, some loose change, crumpled bank-notes, a comb....

Irritated, she watched until she could bear it no longer. "Where you left them. Where you always leave them. In the ignition."

Without a word, he swept the items on the dashboard up and threw them into the glove compartment. To do so, he had to lean across her; as he pulled back, he trailed his hand across her lap and squeezed her thigh.

"Easy now. Be patient with me, li'l English." His voice was so soft, she barely heard him.

"Patient? Well, I won't have to be that much longer." Kathy bit back the words. Everything had been so perfect; she mustn't spoil this bonus of a day he'd given her. Taking a deep breath, she pushed all thought beyond "now" to the back of her mind.

"Let's make the best of what's left," she added briskly, realising she sounded like her Nan. "Even though the weather's done a dirty on us. Shame about missing the tide. We'll just have to go back to the hotel. Everything's closed this time of year."

The windscreen was opaque with moisture, both inside and out. Kathy wiped at it with her sleeve. Before them, the causeway was a thin black ribbon, the sea sliding swiftly across the sand towards it, grey, rough and choppy with white horses, and melding with an indistinguishable horizon, where Holy Island was lying, a long and irregular, faint grey and green blur.

As Joe turned the car round and began to drive them away from the magic of Lindisfarne – now a lost opportunity – Kathy felt she could kick herself. She'd never thought about the tides. Things had been going so amazingly well, she'd expected it all to continue falling into place. At breakfast, the owner of the B&B had been charming, producing the packed lunch they'd asked for and wishing them a lovely day. Sure that the woman must have heard them at it the night before, Kathy had been embarrassed to come down at first. But if she had, there had been no sign of it.

She thought about her plan, now gone awry. She'd imagined them visiting the ruined abbey, walking together under the Rainbow Arch where she would repeat the words he had once said to her about them being a storm and a rainbow. Take him to another castle, and then show him tiny Cuthbert's Island, where she'd planned to tell him about the great patron saint of Northumberland and how he had communed with animals. Stories that probably weren't so different to some of his. She'd racked her brain all the way there, trying to remember Sunday-school stories....

Anything to keep him interested and occupied, she'd thought. At the back of her mind was that they might be caught by the tide and she'd get another night with him.

"You know, they say that Arthur – the king – is only sleeping," Kathy said, trying to shut the idea of his approaching departure away. "That's why he gets called 'the once and only king'. To return, in the hour of his country's need, from where he sleeps: the Isle of Apple Trees. Some people say that's in the south-west of England."

"Yeah, I read that's where he was took when he was so badly wounded. To the Isle of Avalon."

"I like the idea," she said dreamily. "It's somehow comforting, to think so great a figure will come back when we need him most." She looked out through the rain-streaked windows, not seeing what was passing by outside. "Like you," she added, so quietly she knew he would not hear.

She had felt close to him all morning, but now the feeling was fading. Trying to recapture it, she thought back. Last night, something had been different. She was sure he'd come just as she did, only she'd been so wiped out she couldn't be sure. And it was no use asking. He never wanted to speak of things like that; he just shut up like a clam if she tried. Yet something was different. That morning, he hadn't wanted to do anything more than hold her in bed, until she commented that they might miss breakfast. He'd taken her hand over the breakfast table and held it, without words, for several minutes. That had been the nearest he'd come to a public show of affection. He'd been somehow more relaxed, made a couple of jokes. And she'd felt his eyes on her, like he was going to say something important, something special. She'd been careful to be patient, but nothing had come out.

And now it was changing from the best day in her life, to the worst....

Wishing he'd left the day before as he'd planned, Joe gave his attention to his bag and the last few things on the bed. Like a bear in a cave, ready to hibernate, he craved his own company.

"You're makin' it hard on yourself," he said harshly.

"What d'you expect?" Kathy voice was petulant. She bounced onto the bed and thrust her face, pale and wet with tears, into his.

"Not all of us can just shut our feelings down. If they've got any in the first place."

"You knew the situation. Your grief's about yourself." It was a familiar enough scene; he knew how to get through it. Except it wasn't quite the same: hidden deep in his chest, a knife-edge glinted and threatened.

She put her hand on his, as if trying to pin him down. "But it doesn't mean.... You think you're a lone wolf. But everybody needs somebody. You won't talk about options. Why can't you take me with you? Or stay here? There, I've said it. This can't just stop here."

He knew it could never work. White people always needed things, and he had nothing and liked it that way. He tried to make this known.

"Got nothin' to offer."

"That doesn't matter! I don't need anything!" Her voice rose in a wail. "All I want is you."

He just had to go through the motions, like an actor in his own movie. "That's what you say right now, but once the flush wears off – an' it will – you'll change your mind soon enough. We had a good time. Time's come to move on."

He knew he should have just melted away without a word when the moment had given itself. Such as when she had been in the shower, say. But he had had an unusual sense of unfairness about that, and now this emotionality, her rounded, piercing eyes on him was the price he had to pay. It was turning into one of the hardest things he'd ever had to do.

"You're pleased to be getting rid of me!"

"I'm not pleased 'bout anythin' right now." He hardened himself for her next outburst, but she seemed to calm suddenly, sitting back on her heels.

"I can't believe you'll just walk away." She was pleading now. "After all that's happened; after what.... Look, you've not had a smoke in two whole days. And you said you felt different, with me. Something like this.... People hardly ever find something like this, what we have. You can't just walk away from it."

Joe couldn't help but be reminded of what had happened between them: how, unlike the first time when she had somehow seduced it out of him, he had at last been able to let go, to find that ultimate release with her. He felt like he was being split in two: one part dancing its cynical way along the knife-edge, untouched, uncaring; the other cut to the quick, bleeding, but smothered. She must never know.

"See, you shook your head," Kathy cried. "You agree, really. Just 'cause you're older, you think you know all about life, but you don't. You were closed down, then you met me. I rattled the keys and the lights came on and you opened up again."

When he said nothing, she softly added: "I love you, Joe, and I know you love me, even if you can't say it.... I know you're wounded, and tired. But love heals; I believe that. That's why you had to come here, to England, I mean. You said it, remember? Look at the things you've said about this land and how it makes you feel. And how at peace you feel with me. Sometimes, anyway." She hung her head.

He liked her honesty, her self-awareness, which was making it even more difficult. But he retained the mask; he'd come to understand it was a very real part of himself.

Her tears started again. "Oh, I know you think it's childish, but the songs don't keep on about love for nothing, there's got to be something in them."

Joe could feel her eyes on him, in him, seeking out the depths of him. To deflect the probing, he sat down and gently cupped her face with both his hands, using his thumbs to wipe away her tears. "Wise child," he murmured, "throwin' my sensibilities back at me."

It was no good to soften, he knew. She had her whole life ahead of her. His own – half thrown away but with a well-worn familiarity – was what he wanted to go back to.

Shutting away the vulnerable core of himself, he added, "Look at me. I got a daughter 'bout your age. In a few years, you'd look at me an' see an old man: bags under my eyes, face like an old leather boot.... You won't want me then, young thing like you. See," he tweaked his hair, "already goin' grey. My body, it's headin' back into the earth, whilst yours is still sproutin'. You can have kids. All that's behind me."

Kathy grasped his wrists and pressed his hands to her breasts. "It's not what's on the outside. You told me that. D'you think I can go backwards? I can't imagine life without you!"

Unable to resist moving his fingers over the soft pliancy of her breasts, Joe felt the swelling warmth below. He thought of the birthmark on her left hip, shaped like a bird, and the freckles on her shoulders. He wanted her, but his back felt rigid as petrified wood and he couldn't move. She leaned towards him. He smelled coffee and anxiety on her breath. Their foreheads rested against each other in a sort of truce.

She was clearly at a loss. Embarrassed for her, Joe felt his magic and his masks falling away like a tattered blanket. He couldn't think. Too fearful, too guilty, his mind fluttered like a bat in the little space he lived in, the little space he was. Too distraught to speak, he got up and finished packing, moving self-consciously, as if in a dream, his limbs slow and cumbersome.

Finally, he indicated an envelope on the dresser. "There's somethin' to help get you started up anew." Suddenly aware that the gesture might look like a payment, he almost regretted it. "Take it as a gift. An' I fixed it so's the room's yours for as long as you need."

He made the mistake of looking at her. She was looking at him, and her eyes were brimming. He'd never seen them so pale, a phantom of the stormy sea colour raised by their love-making. Ghost eyes. His throat began to constrict.

Knowing the wisdom of not looking into another's eyes, Joe tore his own away, wishing he'd had the sense, the wisdom, to leave with the rest of the crew. One final time, he hardened himself. "Hey, li'l chickadee. You'll be fine. You take care, now."

He couldn't bring himself to touch her and left her sitting

motionless and silent, heading straight out of the hotel, unseeing, bag in hand.

Jamming his foot down on the gas and leaving the little town with a roar and at speed seemed to help. Once he hit the openness of the road, he opened a small window into himself.

Inside was a cavernous emptiness. He was nowhere to be found.

SIX

The stile is old and rickety; the steps creak and complain. Heart in mouth, Kathy sits astride the top strut. The wood quietens. She sees it isn't rotten; it's just that the nails need hammering in properly.

Looking around from her high vantage-point, she is sure she knows where she is, yet something is different. Below, the meadow stretches away, lush and green, down to the stream. At least, she thinks there is a stream, hidden away behind the undulating row of saplings and undergrowth. A movement of air stirs the leaves of the young trees, turning them silver-bellied up.

The faint sound she is hearing cannot easily be identified. At first she thinks it is the whispering of the wind, or music in the distance. Now it seems more like voices, drifting thinly. She looks for their source.

There does not seem to be anyone, anywhere.

Kathy steps down from the stile and walks down towards the hidden stream, using grassy tussocks as stepping-stones when the ground becomes sticky, marshy. As she remembered, the stream is wide, clear and shallow. She can see pebbles on the sandy bed, looking like bubbles about to make their wobbly way to the surface.

There is still no obvious source of the sound, which, she now realises, is a sort of whispering hum. Sometimes it's like voices, softly chanting; the next moment, like instruments, making an angelic but sad sound, a tuneless lifting and falling.

Three old women are sitting on a grassy bank on the far side of the stream. Positive they weren't there when she arrived, Kathy supposes that they are making the sound. It doesn't seem at all odd that they can do it with their mouths closed. Nor that they're wearing almost identical, old-fashioned, pale beige twin-sets and pleated skirts in a plaid. Although it's not really how old ladies would dress in the countryside, it is how her Nan always dresses, she remembers; but then Nan would never have sat on bare ground, like these three are doing.

The one in the middle is looking right at her. Kathy realises it is her Nan, after all; and all three of them are waving for her to come across the water.

She takes off her shoes – brown leather lace-ups, she's vaguely surprised to notice, wondering why she'd worn such ugly things. Before she enters the water, she looks behind her, back up the pasture to the dark wood on the top of the hill. Then, turning her back as if on a disquieting memory, she steps into the water.

Deeper than she anticipated, it is quite warm. Soon she is waist-deep, and the other side is much further away than she thought. In fact, she can't see it at all now; just an endless soft blue, mirror-smooth. There's no difference where the water ends and the sky begins. It doesn't matter in the slightest to her, though. Comfortably, she moves into a lazy breast-stroke. The water seems to gently support her. She feels as if she could swim forever, if she had to.

Except the humming-buzzing sound is changing somehow.

She is on the other side of the stream. Two of the old women have gone. Only her Nan is standing there now, on the bank, frowning, hands on her hips.

It makes little sense to Kathy. She feels afraid; usually Nan is smiling and kindly. Then to her horror, her Nan shudders briefly and seems to go through some kind of change, the colour in her face draining away so she looks ill, just as the strange humming song – or music, or whatever – stops, although echoes of it linger in Kathy's mind.

The white-faced old woman rocks on her feet; she's gesturing, pointing, as if she's telling Kathy which way to go. Upstream, it seems.

"Take the hollow way."

Kathy hears the words inside her head. It was her Nan's voice, although she never saw her mouth move.

There is a steep ascent, and no indication of any "way"; just a jumble of rocks and boulders below an overhanging cliff. The source of the stream, a silvery sliver threading its way down, is now evident.

Kathy is aware that home is in the other direction.

"Nan, are you okay?" Her voice sounds loud in her own ears.

The old woman is gone. Somehow that doesn't seem strange, but the recollection of what happens when she doesn't do as Nan says makes Kathy begin the walk upwards. Weaving between the rocks, she finds a faint path and with surprising ease, is on top of the cliff.

Trees crowd thickly up to the edge, except for in front of her: she is in a small grassy clearing containing a stone tower. Thinking it could be some kind of observation point, she approaches the wooden door at its base.

A slight movement at one of the higher apertures catches her eye. Not a reflection, she realises; there's no glass in any of the narrow slits, which look more like places from which to fire an arrow than enjoy the view.

The door is open. Inside is a round room, empty but for a scattering of dusty, skeletal leaves. At the far side is a shadowy opening, from which a spiral staircase, carved from stone, disappears upwards. She begins to climb it, one hand on the wall as much for reassurance and guidance as support; the light in the stairwell is poor and the steps are narrow and steep, pitted and worn. She winds upwards, round and round, for an age, and emerges into sunlight.

From the top of the tower, the woods stretch as far as she can see on all sides, green and unbroken, like a carpet. Directly below, in the clearing in front of the door, she sees figures and some horses, saddled and bridled.

Ducking back out of view, Kathy is suddenly afraid. She must have been seen; she is trespassing and the owners of the place have come to deal with her. There is nowhere to hide. Wondering what possessed her to come here in the first place, she makes her way back down and in no time at all, is at the bottom of the staircase. Her heart drops into her stomach.

A dark figure blocks the brightness of the open doorway. Cloaked and helmeted, its long, black shadow flung across the flag-stoned floor almost to her feet, it is sinister, threatening. Her instinct is to run, but there's nowhere to go except back up the stairs. She's trapped.

Yet something about the figure, which doesn't move nor say a thing, is familiar.

Kathy realises it's not a cloak, but a long coat. Not a helmet, but a hat.

It is Joe who is standing in the doorway.

A warm, bubbly feeling fills her body. She can hardly believe her eyes. What is he doing here? Surely he's not the owner? This is beyond her wildest dream.

Then a thought strikes her: Is this a dream? To be sure it isn't, she gives her arm a little pinch and feels a slight, sharp pain. Flooded with delight, she hardly knows what to do with herself.

This is real, she thinks. It's true. He's come back. Thrilling with excitement, she gives a little cry.

And not only is it Joe, he's happy to see her, his teeth white against his dark skin, his familiar, almond-shaped eyes crinkling at the edges, meeting hers, soft and melting-warm, exactly as she remembers.

"It had to be something that would make you see," he is saying.

"I knew it," she says, dizzy with feeling. "It's just that I needed help to get here."

He opens his arms and she rushes forward, ready to melt into them. Into him....

"Geroff."

The low growl startled Kathy. The voice was not Joe's. And the light, it was so bright it hurt her eyes. In the split second it took to register the open curtains, it hit her: it had only been a dream, after all. Another stupid dream. And she'd really thought she'd managed to get over him.

Rubbing her eyes, the wonderful, tingly feeling draining swiftly away, she sat up and looked down at the tousled brown hair and scowling face of Tim.

"Christ, you're all over me like a rash," he muttered sleepily, turning over and pulling the duvet with him. "What's the matter with you? You've been thrashing about, moaning and muttering stuff, making no sense. I need my sleep. Got to finish that report before I go back."

Cold disappointment bit deep into Kathy, keeping her from retorting. She got up for a drink of water and when she got back, he was fast asleep again, which didn't help. Roughly jerking back the duvet, she lay down and curled up in a foetal shape, her back to him. After a few minutes, her body jangling with emotions, too wide-awake to think of going back to sleep, she turned on her back and lay staring unseeing at the ceiling.

Angrily, she thought about how she'd managed to go for two whole days without Joe once entering her head. It had taken long enough. Weeks. Then just when she thought she was getting somewhere, a dream like this. Why now?

Yet, closing her eyes, Kathy couldn't resist going back into the dream.

How amazingly real it had felt: the warm and soothing water; the strange appearance of her Nan; then the bursting-happy moment she knew it was Joe. She could still see the way he'd smiled; his eyes, darker and more velvety-warm than ever, meeting hers so directly. It had been the most wonderful and deep connection. Like soul-mates, about to melt into each other, she thought, feeling the tingly-warmth returning just from the memory of it. The setting had been like something from the movie, she realised; a place he might have chosen. She wished she could put the dream on rewind and go back into it; live in it; or at least through what happened next.

If only bloody idiot Tim hadn't woken her. Tears pricked at her eyes. Even though she knew better and was aware of what she was doing to herself, she got up again and padded barefoot and naked over to the chest of drawers. Opening the bottom one, she rummaged under her jumpers and pulled out a framed photograph.

Something of his essence had been caught: lips pursed as they did when his mind was somewhere else; his eyes looking somewhere beyond the photographer; his dark hair sleeked back, the pony-tail curling over the collar of his black coat. Beyond him, a blurred hint of the vast grey-green expanse of the moors beneath a pale sky.

She remembered how thrilled she'd been when the photographer who was doing the stills had given it to her, right at the end of the last shoot. She'd been so grateful; once Joe had gone, all she had to remember him by was his pendant, now buried in a shoebox at the back of the wardrobe, and this picture, her main point of reference once she realised she was having a hard time remembering what he looked like.

But she wanted to forget. She hated him for making her fall in love with him, then leaving her in the lurch; for giving her a taste of how it might be, then snatching it away; hated that she'd kept the photo when she should have ripped it to shreds; hated that she'd had to get it out again.

Thrusting the image back into the drawer as if it repelled her, Kathy made herself remember the bleakness of the terrible days after he had gone: the emptiness; crying till she could hardly breathe; the bruised feeling in her chest. A broken heart, she was sure. She had filled the time writing sad little poems on hotel note-paper, sitting by the phone, driving herself crazy, unable to eat, waiting for him to come back or at least ring her. He'd given her no phone number in London, and she'd known he was there only for a short while, but she'd still fantasised about following him there, and then when she knew he must be back in Los Angeles, imagined getting on a plane to America and simply turning up at the studio. He had left her enough money to do that and she had tortured herself, wondering if that might have been in his mind when he gave it to her.

But in the end, all she had done was crawl back home. Hating herself for it, it had seemed to take up the last of her strength; her life had caved in on itself and she had retreated to her room for days to avoid the crude jibes of the men and a mother who cared yet had little to offer but well-meaning platitudes. Her life had felt utterly ruined.

Eventually, the lack of any contact from Joe, coupled with the stress of being at home all the time, had brought her out of it. She knew she had to get on with her life; even he had said that. And although she hadn't wanted to use it, the money he'd given her had made it possible, even easy. It had been more than enough for a deposit and the first month's rent on the flat-share in Newcastle. Getting that sorted and starting a new job as a receptionist in a busy accountancy practice had kept her so occupied that she'd had little time to think.

Seeing Tim again had seemed the best way to wipe Joe's memory from her mind and her body. She'd known he'd want to have sex, and doing it with someone familiar had seemed like a good idea at the time; someone new would have been unthinkable. Even so, it had felt like a betrayal, a pollution of something precious. The slobbery insensitive kisses. She'd almost thrown up when he'd poked his tongue into her mouth. And the rest; she'd just shut herself away and got on with it....

A strangely familiar sound interrupted her scattered thoughts. Kathy held her breath.

It was the whispering almost-song in her dream.

It was Tim, fast asleep on his back, breathing loudly through his mouth. The magical music in the dream, calling her, had been nothing but the idiot's stupid wheezing, leaking into her sleeping mind. Kathy felt like she could strangle him. She almost shoved him out of the bed.

That'd show him, she thought with a fresh surge of resentment; telling her she was like a rash, when he should be grateful to be with her. Shallow airhead; no good at sex; no consideration; no poetry in him at all. She felt sick that she'd even allowed him near her, when with Caz, her flat-mate, away at her parents', she could have had the whole place to herself for the weekend.

Kathy saw now how lonely, how desperate she'd been. And too soft.

That's what her Nan had always used to say, she remembered, thinking of how she'd been in the dream, too, at the place they used to go for picnics when she was little. Telling her what to do, as always. Although of course, Nan had been gone for years. That's probably why her dreaming mind had turned Nan into a sad ghost, she realised.

She wondered about "hollow way", and promised herself she'd look it up.

Closing her eyes, unable to resist returning to the last few heady moments of the dream, Kathy recalled the strength of her feelings as she saw Joe: the flood of relief, of love. And his eyes; the recognition had been so true, so deep. How could it be, she thought, that something that felt so real, even as far as a pinch, could only be a dream? It was so unfair. Would she ever get rid of her silly, childish idea that there was such a thing as The One?

Decisively, she took the picture out again and removed the photograph from its frame.

It was well past time. Wishing she could erase his memory as easily as she could tear it up, she stared at Joe's image, willing herself not to feel anything. Reflexively, she clutched at her belly; despite her determination, tears filled her eyes.

For one last time, she closed her eyes and directed her thought, visualising it heading up out of the flat, into the sky above the city then whizzing across the Atlantic and the American continent to land somewhere in the region she believed he lived. She imagined it striking into his temple, the same one she'd massaged when he'd been getting one of his migraines and she'd stopped it from happening.

You'll never forget me, she thought, fiercely concentrating. You'll never be at peace without me.

The doorbell rang. A wild and irrational hope made her leap up and rush to pull some clothes on so she could answer it.

Redness fills his eyes, then slowly clears. The misshapen figure lying on the sand might be an old drunk, or a corpse. A dust-devil begins to form, snatching up brush and sticks in a macabre, spiralling dance before losing interest and dropping away in an arroyo.

Joe looks up at the sky. Cloudless, it is a sickly yellow. Like a mirage, the land shimmers, the sharp edges of it softening, then reforming, arid and broken.

No-one comes out into the badlands without good reason, he knows.

As if pulled by a rope, Joe finds himself running behind a dark figure on horseback. He is leaving no tracks, so knows this is a special trail he is on. The figure has dark-blue ripples running down its back, and two faces: a man's looking forward, a woman's looking back. Racing now, the wind in his hair and a moaning in his ears, Joe sees a myriad of snakes curving along beside him, sinuous and sleek.

Fear tightens his throat. He has always been wary of snakes. But they don't seem like they will bite. Intent on their progress, heads slightly raised, they are taking no notice of him at all; not even the ones that somehow pass between his feet without tripping him up. He wants to cry to the dark figure to slow; to stop this mad, head-long flight. But when he opens his mouth, his words are snatched and scattered by the wind.

Now he is riding the horse, the thundering of its hooves ringing in his ears. Joe leans into its neck, urging it forward. It is getting darker, and the wind is howling. But the horse is faltering. It falls, and dies.

He is very sad, knows it must be his fault for pushing the animal too hard. He buries it in the place where it has fallen, covering it with rocks to protect it from wild animals.

The red sand seems to shift and stir, as if the snakes are writhing just below the surface. Mesmerised, Joe watches the sinuous movement. The grains begin to act like prisms, forming a twisting kaleidoscope of rainbow colours. They rise, and whirl like water in a pot. Another dust-devil, only he is somehow in it. It becomes unbearable and he has to look away.

The land is fading ... not fading, but becoming paler, slowly leached of colour: the rocks, pale grey; sand, almost white; scrubby vegetation, a washed-out green. Even the sky is drained of colour.

An old man, his lined face burned by the wind and covered with grease, is conducting some weird kind of rite: chanting a song and taking off his clothes and painting his body. Joe looks down; it would not be right to watch. He sees he too is naked, and it is actually his own body the old man is painting, using a stone knife. He realises he is much bruised, and the old man is painting over the bruises, still chanting. Then the old man is painting him breasts. Although that seems odd, he must accept whatever the wisdom of the old man decrees.

A pain runs through Joe's gut. He squats down and gives birth to a child. It slips out of him, not much bigger than a frog, pale yellow-green, but otherwise perfect in every way. He is devastated; everything seems hopeless. How can a small child survive in such a desolate place? Yet it seems to live. His chest aches with relief as he remembers the breasts the old man gave him.

"Tell the lie three times; be locked into it forever." A sing-song tone. The words might have come from the old man, but he is nowhere to be seen.

The moon is bright, its cold, clear light silvering the desolate land. Slow and hunched, a figure is approaching from across the mesa. Somehow he knows it is her, long before he sees her face.

How Kathy found her way here, with no-one to guide her, not even a trail to follow, he cannot imagine. She is pale with exhaustion, her dark-blue blouse and voluminous skirt stained and dusty. She seems to trip and stumble, and the small bundle she is carrying falls to the earth.

Thinking she must be exhausted by the walk and the heat, he hurries to her and is about to touch her, but she shrinks away. She is trembling.

She is afraid.

He remembers he is naked, and wonders: what am I in her eyes?

"It's okay," Joe speaks gently. He realises he too is trembling. "We can go rest."

Her face is soft, and solemn. Her eyes meet his. Misted, sad, they remind him of the sea in winter. Locked into his, they darken like an approaching storm. He'd forgotten how beautiful her hair is, wants to stroke the red-gold shining tendrils. But as he reaches out, she sighs and looks down.

Deep red drops spatter the pale sand around her feet.

"Oh, no!" Joe cries. Forgetting his earlier fear, he embraces her.

For a moment, the recognition of her body, the familiar smell of wet earth and wood, almost overwhelms him. But she's like a twig; he's afraid he will break her. And her body holds no warmth. No matter how close he holds her, even though she's folded deep in his embrace, he cannot warm her. She is cold as death.

He begins to cry. Through his tears, the land is a ghostly blur; not red but grey-green. A furnace roars in his belly, his groin. Sweat begins to trickle down his back. If only he could give her some of this excessive heat.

"Take the stone from your mouth." The voice is filled with contempt.

Wondering how the old man knew it was there when he didn't himself, Joe spits it out into his hand. It is shaped like a tooth, jagged and brown. Feeling more small objects in his mouth, he spits again and again, until all his teeth lie cupped in his palm, brown and rotten. He wonders how he'll look without them, how he'll chew food, but, running his tongue over the empty gums, he can feel the sharp edges of new teeth, growing in their place.

He can carry her to safety. "I must go back and get my shoes. The ground is very rough." But when he gets them, he sees they are the moccasins he wore when he was about six or seven years old.

When he returns, Kathy is nowhere to be seen.

Desperately wanting to tell her about the moccasins, he goes running off to find her, and impales himself on a piece of iron that is sticking out of a great rock. It pierces his chest, right between the painted breasts, with the sickening sound of metal tearing through bone, muscle, gristle.

Distraught that he has to die just when everything is coming right, Joe finds he is back in his trailer. The old man is there too, wrapped in a robe. Joe wants to be alone when he dies, but he cannot speak. He can barely hear the whispering: "Listen for Nlch'i, the wind-that-sings, the breath of life lost in the dark of time." As the old man's words settle inside his mind, somewhere deep inside the encroaching darkness of death, Joe finds meaning.

This dream stayed with him all day. Vivid, real and unreal, it left Joe feeling mangled, bringing back things he tried not to let himself think about in his waking hours.

Winding up the movie had kept his mind occupied; he'd made sure of that. Sure, there'd been the occasional moments, triggered by the trace of her smell on his clothes, wisps of dreams. All of which could be kept under control by getting up the moment he woke and keeping busy until sleep hit him again. And by not toking up. That, he'd found, had not helped at all, taking him back in his mind to places where he knew better than to go. By staying away from the smoke, he didn't drift. By filling his mind with work, the dreams stayed away.

The wide emptiness of the mesa lay spread out before him like a threadbare blanket.

It had been good to come back, but the space gave his mind the opportunity to roam. And that the English girl should still be so strong in his mind after all this time was not something he'd anticipated.

Despite himself, Joe found himself returning again and again to the dream-images. The traditional clothing she'd been wearing had been a neat touch, he thought. He remembered her eyes, their pale clarity; in the dream, darkening, electric. Yet the colour of her hair had been like that of the English queen, Guinevere. And somehow, that distant northern landscape, so dull and cold, had leaked through his own. Why had the girl been so cold? And what did the blood-spots mean? Was she safe? And the embrace: fraught, yet moving him more than he at first had recognised. He recalled how she'd changed her whole life just to spend those few days with him.

As the sun set in a vermilion smear and darkness spread its wings, early stars dusted the deepening, velvety vastness of the sky. Joe sat out on the deck of his trailer, playing his flute and indulging himself in memory: the gentle flare of her hips; her long legs; her smooth belly, glistening with fine, blonde hairs. Alone with the dying wind, the yipping of the local pack of coyotes a chorus to the sad sound he was creating, he rocked, closing his eyes and recalling those long legs wrapped round him; the sweet saltiness of her skin; her warm and welcoming, tight moistness. He remembered the kick it had given him to see her sitting in his chair on the set, wrapped in his blanket.

He recalled her land: the great empty spaces so like yet so unlike his own. The moors, grey with falling rain. The graphite, corrugated North Sea, torn and bleeding white. The biting winds from the east, carrying messages from lands, places even deeper in the beyond than he might go in this life.

She'd lightened the open loneliness of that faraway northern land, dark and cold, wet and wild.

Joe had always thought he never looked back; never missed anything, anywhere, anyone, once they were behind him. But the wind had been strong in the night, singing its song, carrying its memories. And, colouring his dream, helping him realise what he'd known but never let himself see: he missed her. He'd never known anything like it. She was in him, some kind of ghost-presence, deep within his bones.

A couple of times, he thought about visiting his second father, his mother's brother, now old and infirm, but one who still chose to live in a hogan, and the one who was always ready to help if something troubled him. But it was hard to imagine returning on the wings of yet another dream, even if he was unsure about some of the images his mind had conjured up. What would he be told that was new?

And then it came clear. He knew what his soul was telling him: he had to face up to himself. Seeming to call for some kind of resolution, the message rising from the depths of him was clear enough.

"The person I was before I met her, is different to the person I am now."

That night, he slept through, untroubled by any dreams.

SEVEN

Ragged banners of cloud raced across the clear sky. Risen early, the moon, a slender white hook, hung low over the horizon. The sunlight poured down in streams. Shimmering and undulating, the land stretched over hill and vale, accommodating the rough and gusting, life-sharing wind.

It blew in Kathy's face and whipped her hair into her eyes. Tucking wayward strands behind her ears, she followed a deer-trod trail between the trees, negotiating scrubby undergrowth and tangles of dead brambles, long and whiplike. Behind her, the wooded valley was tinged with the faintest touch of green, the river running brown and slow eastwards towards the sea. Thrusting branches aside, she saw she was now just below the abbey.

Although she wanted to, she didn't dare go inside. There was a small house where a caretaker lived and she didn't want a confrontation. Not for the first time, she wished she'd planned better: acting on the spur of the moment, she hadn't thought to get a pass into Hulne Park. And it had been no picnic, so far. Hitching a ride had taken longer than she'd anticipated; the road was not well-travelled. She'd had to walk over a mile before being picked up by a friendly farmer, who'd dropped her off at the big double gates; a private entrance, she knew, but the one nearest the abbey.

They had been closed, forbiddingly, but luckily were well-oiled. Heart in her mouth, she'd had to sneak past the keeper's lodge and walk the first half-mile briskly, as there were no trees to hide behind. But no-one had challenged her. Then she'd turned down into the woods, to avoid the paved road. They were private lands, after all.

But she really wished she could spend some time among the abbey ruins. She knew them intimately; every year throughout her childhood, the annual Sunday-school picnic had been spent there. It hadn't been about the silly children's games the vicar had organised, or the food, but something about the feeling of the place and its many secret hiding-places. Glad to have a day out, her mother had let her go her own way, leaving Kathy to the private games of her imagination. The old stone statues of monks dotted about the place had added to its atmosphere, although they had scared her a little at the time. She'd used to imagine that they came to life when no-one was there, and that one day she might turn a corner and catch one of them, moving about his duties, and he'd turn on her with a growl, like a bear. One was especially spooky: the one praying to the heavens, his mouth open as if he were howling, like an animal.

As the image filled her mind's eye, Kathy gave a sudden gasp. It had just struck her: that was how she had been feeling, all those weeks of trying to get over Joe. She'd been in agony. It was as if the monk's desperate prayer, ripped from his heart, were her own.

Excited by this realisation, she pulled off her leather shoulder-bag. Taking out a notebook and pencil, she made a few notes. Then, after a drink from her water-bottle, she tried to work out exactly where she was, using the gateway and tower beside it as a marker. Glad of the decent weather, she fleetingly wondered if she was being too silly and romantic. But it was too late for thoughts like that. She began to skirt the bottom edge of the hill, keeping the tower of the abbey above her in sight, a watchful and, she liked to think, guiding presence. Finding a gap in the hedge, she re-entered the woods.

Everything seemed different under the bright sunlight. Methodically, she began a weaving search, sure she was close.

Protected from the wind, the trees were still, although she could still hear the soughing and swooshing higher up. Fallen logs seemed to be everywhere; she'd forgotten what a messy place a wildwood was. When she actually found the little clearing, she could hardly believe her luck; she only recognised it because the log had an odd fork in the end of it, like a large and rounded, raised snake's tongue.

Positive it had been bigger, she looked at it for a long while, trying to recall the soft sad sound that had drawn her here. It was only a few weeks ago, but it seemed like another life; a lifetime ago. Above her, the wind gently wandered among bare branches beginning to swell with buds. She listened, as if it might remind her of the sound she was seeking.

The entrancing song of the magic flute, which had drawn her to him.

Now that she'd actually found the place, Kathy knew it had been worth it. Sitting down on the rotting log, as near to the exact place she had sat, heart in mouth, not all that long ago, she looked along it, trying to recall exactly where and how he had been sitting, in his black coat and hat; the pony-tail....

After a while, she opened her bag and took out a plastic folder. From it, she pulled out a photo. It looked a little battered, and had been torn and sellotaped up again.

Kathy looked at it for a long time. She found she wasn't really thinking; her thoughts skated across the surface of her mind like water-boatmen across the surface of a pond. She remembered snatches of scenes and conversation, like an old film being played back erratically. When she focussed on the picture of Joe again, she understood why she had wanted to come here.

Here she was, at the place of beginning. Because this was about an ending, and a new beginning. She lost all sense of urgency, wishing to savour these moments. Even when the thought of her Mam popped into her head, it was only for long enough for her to give a slight shake of her head.

Putting the photo on the log beside her, she returned to the bag and drew out her notebook again. Sifting through the pages, she chose one and began to read out loud:

"Dark Raven, Fair Lily

A sad song was his, song of a wayfarer
lost in thunder cloud and lightning flash,
son of the dark wind,
but with magic dancing at his fingertips
he called in the rainbow.

Hers was a small song, barely born;
alone in the tower she lingered,
pale and wan, echoing the ocean;
but the morning mist melted away
with the rising of the sun."

As the words fell away, she frowned a little, then rummaged for her pencil and scribbled something in the margin. For a few more minutes she wrote, then just sat and reflected for a while until her eyes closed.

The sun sank slowly in the sky and the air cooled.

Kathy started. She didn't think she'd fallen asleep, but now she was chilled. Her little book of poems was still in her hand; Joe's photo beside her. She gave his image a kiss, then slid it back into the folder and pulled out an envelope.

Holding it as if it were some rare and precious manuscript, she studied the front of it as if there might be some code hidden among the simple typescript, the postmark, the stamp with an American flag. Heart fluttering at the back of her throat, she slipped her thumb inside and pulled out the airline ticket.

Only three days to go.

ACKNOWLEDGEMENTS

Permission to quote from "The Half-Remarkable Question" by Robin Williamson, *Wee Tam*, The Incredible String Band, 1968, is gratefully acknowledged. Thank you, Robin, poetic mentor.

For his sensitive creation of the book cover illustration, I extend my thanks and appreciation to Yuri Leitch. (www.yurileitch.co.uk)

My deepest thanks to my publisher, Ian Thorp, for his dedication and commitment to this new edition of *A Dark Wind*.

For her significant artistic suggestion, I bless my daughter Sivan.

As ever, I am deeply grateful for the heartfelt encouragement and loving support of my beloved husband Anthony.

A native of the county of Northumberland, England, Celia's deep, personal interest in the North American Indian has been part of her make-up for as long as she can remember. After completing her education in the UK, she spent several years in Jerusalem, Israel, before immigrating to British Columbia, Canada, where she lived for eighteen years, working in publishing and education, and where her three children were born.

In the critical period of her mid-life, Celia was involved for six years in cultural preservation with tribal members of the Sinixt Nation of Canada, as they began their return to their tribal identity. Her memoir of this extraordinary experience, *A Twist in Coyote's Tale*, has been adapted into a film, due for release in 2010.

Now living with her husband in the West Country of England, where she works to revitalise her own indigenous roots, Celia is currently writing a saga set in ancient North America. When not planning her writing on long dog-walks, she can usually be found tending her beautiful woodland chakra garden.

For more information about the author's activities, please visit her website: www.earthskywalk.com

Lightning Source UK Ltd.
Milton Keynes UK
28 August 2009

143152UK00001B/27/P